THE SCARY BOOK OF Fairy Tales

The Scary Book of Fairy Tales

13-Digit ISBN: 978-1-40035-228-9

10-Digit ISBN: 1-40035-228-2

Books published by Cider Mill Press Book Publishers are available at special discounts for bulk purchases in the United States by corporations, institutions, and other organizations. For more information, please contact the publisher.

Cider Mill Press Book Publishers
"Where good books are ready for press"
501 Nelson Place
Nashville, Tennessee 37214, USA
cidermillpress.com

HarperCollins Publishers, Macken House, 39/40 Mayor Street Upper, Dublin 1, D01 C9W8, Ireland (https://www.harpercollins.com)

Typography: Brokenscript OT, HWT Aetna, Meno Text

Printed in Bosnia & Herzegovina

25 26 27 28 29 GPS 5 4 3 2 1

First Edition

THE SCARY BOOK OF Fairy Tales

You Won't Find Happily Ever After Here

Tim Rayborn

Illustrations by Neil Evans

CIDER MILL PRESS BOOK PUBLISHERS

Table of Contents

Introduction 7

Snow White (Brothers Grimm) 10

Aschenputtel, the Little Cinder Girl (Brothers Grimm) 14

Hansel and Gretel (Brothers Grimm) 18

Rapunzel (Brothers Grimm) 21

Rumpelstiltskin (Brothers Grimm) 25

The Children of Hameln (Brothers Grimm) 28

The Juniper Tree (Brothers Grimm) 31

Herr Korbes (Brothers Grimm) 33

Frau Trude (Brothers Grimm) 35

The Three Army Surgeons (Brothers Grimm) 38

The Strange Feast (Brothers Grimm) 41

The Robber Bridegroom (Brothers Grimm) 42

The Ungrateful Son (Brothers Grimm) 44

The Goose Girl (Brothers Grimm) 47

Fitcher's Bird (Brothers Grimm) 51

How Some Children Played at Slaughtering (Brothers Grimm) 54

Mother Holle (Brothers Grimm) 56

The Girl Without Hands (Brothers Grimm) 57

The Little Mermaid (Hans Christian Andersen) 60

The Red Shoes (Hans Christian Andersen) 63

The Story of the Thumb Sucker
(Heinrich Hoffmann, *Der Struwwelpeter*, 1845) 66

The Very Sad Tale with the Matches
(Heinrich Hoffmann, *Der Struwwelpeter*, 1845) 67

The Flea (Giambattista Basile, the *Pentamerone*, 1634) 69

Penta of the Chopped-Off Hands
(Giambattista Basile, the *Pentamerone*, 1634) 72

Little Red Riding Hood
(Charles Perrault, *Histoires ou contes du temps passé*, 1697) 75

Blue Beard
(Charles Perrault, *Histoires ou contes du temps passé*, 1697) 79

Donkeyskin
(Charles Perrault, *Histoires ou contes du temps passé*, 1697) 83

The Crucifix Priest (Medieval French *fabliaux*) 86

The Story of the Three Bears (Robert Southey, 1839) 87

Vasilisa and Baba Yaga (Russian fairy tale) 90

Tatterhood (Norwegian fairy tale) 95

The Satin Frock (Yorkshire folktale) 97

My Mother in the Fold (Icelandic folktale) 99

The Plague Swarm (Polish folktale) 101

The Two Corpses (Russian folktale) 105

The Snow Child (French/German folktale) 106

The Griffin's Feather and the Speaking Bone
(Italian folktale) 109

The Enchanted Pig (Romanian folktale).....................................111

The Tale of Scheherazade (*1001 Nights*).....................................114

The Merchant and the Two Sharpers (*1001 Nights*)................116

The Place Where There Were No Graves
(Egyptian folktale) 117

The Foolish Friend (The *Panchatantra*, Indian folktale)..................119

The Daughter Who Married a Skull (Nigerian folktale) 121

Botan Dōrō, the Peony Lantern (Japanese folktale) 125

Hailibu, the Hunter (Mongolian folktale) 127

The Boy Devoured by a Stone
(Tinguian folktale, Philippines) 130

The Old Woman Who Was Kind to Insects
(Inuit folktale) 132

The Timbo Tree (Guaraní folktale, Paraguay)............................ 134

Boitatá (South American/Brazilian legend) 135

La Llorona (Mexican and Central American ghost story) 138

About the Author 143

Introduction

Ah, the magical world of fairy tales! So whimsical, so sweet, so charming, so...violent and bloodthirsty? Most of us listened to fairy tales as young children, and many might have had their introduction to them via Disney or other child-friendly versions. Tales like Snow White, Cinderella, and Rapunzel are timeless classics that transport young listeners into fantasy worlds of young love, adventure, evildoers, strange creatures, and more.

But there is a much darker side to many of these beloved tales than most people realize. And many of these darker tales were found in the original collections themselves. The famous tales collected by Jacob and Wilhelm Grimm are the most obvious examples. Indeed, a few of these stories, which they collected from various tellers in early nineteenth-century Germany, were so dark and depressing that they removed or modified them in later editions.

Stories of murder, cannibalism, incest, torture, kidnapping, and more abound in these allegedly children's tales. But why is that? Why are some of them so horrible? Well, these kinds of fairy tales were often intended as teaching tools for young children. Warning them about a cannibalistic witch who lived in a nearby forest was a good way to show them the peril of wandering off on their own. The world had plenty of its own very real dangers, then and now, and impressing on a child from a young age not to talk to strangers, or get lost somewhere, was valuable for keeping them safe. Cloaking these dangers in fantastical stories only made them more meaningful.

It's fair to say that the times in which these stories arose were more violent, people's lifespans tended to be shorter, and their lives were harder overall. Children were not coddled and often had to grow up much more quickly, especially those who were poor. So, a tale that offered some important lesson or gave a reason for why certain things were the way they were made good sense. And often, these stories used very violent and bloody examples!

You might be wondering what the difference is between a fairy tale (or a fairy story, as the British call them) and a folktale. That's a very good question, and folkloric scholars have been arguing about it for ages. Most of the key elements of fairy tales (magic, animals, happy endings, evil witches, curses, etc.) can also be found in the broader category of folktales. Some scholars have argued that early male anthropologists used the designation "fairy tale" in an almost dismissive way, to play down the importance of such tales, passed on largely from mothers and grandmothers to children, as opposed to the more "elevated" myths that these anthropologists collected and studied in their lofty academic halls. There is certainly some truth in this. In any case, the debate will probably not be settled soon.

This book contains classic European fairy tales (from the Brothers Grimm, Hans Christian Andersen, and others) as well as stories that are considered to be more in the category of folktales from all over the world. What unites them is their dedication to the violent, the bloody, the treacherous, the repulsive, and the "OMG, are you kidding me?" Some are shocking, some are appalling, but they all offer amazing insights into the human need for stories that plunge into the darker depths of our minds, even while, in theory, offering these stories up as entertainment for children.

You will know many of these stories (especially the Grimms' tales), but you might not have heard these versions before. Sometimes the earliest renderings of the tales are a good deal darker than later ones. Eagle-eyed readers will also notice that some stories have similar motifs: blood dropping into snow, a girl losing her hands, vindictive and wicked stepmothers, miscommunication in letters to and from kings, warnings not to go into certain places in a house, cannibalistic old ladies, and so on. These examples show that often such stories grew out of stock traditions that were later embellished and changed to suit the needs of a given storyteller and his or her audience.

Also, in a lot of these stories, the women don't fare as well as our modern sensibilities would like them to. Daughters are promised in marriage without any obvious consent on their part, or young women are the victims of violence and abuse. And people tend to fall in love and want to get married at an absurdly quick pace. But in many cases, these heroines do come out on top, vanquishing the evils that try to stop them. And while the young are often beautiful and good while the old are nasty and evil, there are stories of horrid young people and kindly elderly folks as well.

Fairy tales continue to enchant us, even into adulthood. While these particular stories aren't exactly what one would call "enchanting," they do allow us a glimpse into the magical worlds of our deeper and darker imaginations, to see both the good and the bad. So, dip into these wonderful stories you thought you knew and prepare to be shocked, disgusted, and disturbed!

Snow White

(Brothers Grimm)

Once, during a cold and snowy winter, a queen sat and embroidered. She happened to prick her finger, and three drops of blood fell into the snow. She wished for a daughter then, as white as the snow, as red as her blood, and as black as her embroidery frame. And soon, she had a daughter with white skin, red lips, and black hair. She named the baby Snow White and then died. Soon, her father the king took another wife, who was beautiful, but proud and cruel. She had a magical looking glass, and she would stand in front of it and ask, "Looking-glass upon the wall, who is fairest of us all?" And it would answer, "You are fairest of them all."

But as Snow White grew up, she became ever more beautiful. And when the queen asked who was fairest, the mirror had to answer that it was Snow White. The queen grew enraged with jealousy and asked a huntsman to take Snow White out into the forest and kill her. But he could not bear to murder her, so he sent her away, hoping the woods would do her in. He shot and killed a boar and took the heart to the queen, who cooked, salted, and ate it, confident that she had devoured Snow White's own heart.

Meanwhile, Snow White wandered in fear until she came to a tiny house. Everything in it was small and in sevens: seven place settings on the table, seven chairs, and seven beds. She helped herself to some food (but not too much) and settled into one of the beds to sleep, for she was very tired. Soon, the house's inhabitants—seven dwarfs—came home, and they saw that their dwelling had been disturbed. And they saw little Snow White in a bed, and though they rejoiced, they didn't wake her.

When she woke in the morning, she was afraid, but after telling them her tale, they replied that if she would help with the chores, she could stay with them for as long as she wished. And so, she worked around the house while they went to a mountain each day to mine for gold. But they warned her that her stepmother might learn the truth, so she should let no one into the house while they were away.

And indeed, when the queen again asked her looking glass who was the fairest, the mirror told her that Snow White, who now lived with seven dwarfs, was the fairest. The queen again flew into a rage. She disguised herself as an old peddler and sought out the seven dwarfs' home. Snow White, thinking that nothing was wrong, opened the door to her. The queen managed to convince her to try on some lace, and when she did, the older woman strangled her. "You are done with being the fairest," the queen declared.

When the dwarfs came home and found her, they cried out, but they cut the lace from her neck and revived her. And when the queen again asked her mirror, it could only tell her that Snow White was still the fairest. She resolved to go back, now disguised as a different old woman. She crafted a poison comb, and convinced Show White to try it. As she combed her hair, she fell down, lifeless. And again, the queen went away, satisfied. But once more, the dwarfs came home and, removing the comb from her hair, revived her. And again, the mirror told the queen the truth.

Shaking with fury, she created a poisoned apple and disguising herself once more; she went to the home of the dwarfs and convinced Snow White to have a bite of it. After she did, she fell to the ground, as if dead, and the queen knew that this time, the dwarfs would not be able to revive her. Indeed, when she asked the mirror once more who was the fairest, it at last told her that it was she.

The dwarfs tried everything to revive Snow White, but their efforts were all in vain. So, they laid her on a bier and wept, for she seemed to be truly dead. They fashioned a coffin with clear glass on the top, and laid her in it, noting that she was a king's daughter. They and all the forest animals mourned her.

But one day, a prince rode through and, seeing the coffin, he asked the dwarfs about this princess. He asked them to give the coffin to him, that he might honor her, and after some time, they were persuaded. He called for his servants to bear it away on their shoulders, but as they walked, one of them stumbled and the coffin lurched forward. At that moment, the piece of poisoned apple caught in Snow White's throat disgorged. She opened her eyes, pushed open the lid, and sat up.

The prince and the dwarfs were overjoyed. They explained what had happened, and the prince offered to take her to his palace, for he longed to marry her. She agreed, and soon they were wed in a glorious ceremony.

Now, they had also invited Snow White's stepmother to the wedding feast, and she dressed herself most regally. And the looking glass could only tell her the truth. Again, she became angry, but she still attended the party to see for herself if Snow White truly was the bride. But once there, the prince's servants seized the queen and placed her in red-hot iron shoes. These were so painful that she tried to dance about to rid herself of them, but she could not, and so she pranced in agony until she dropped dead.

Aschenputtel, the Little Cinder Girl

(Brothers Grimm)

Once, a rich man had a wife who was dying. She called her daughter to her and made her promise to be good, saying she would look down on her from heaven. In time, her father married another woman, but this stepmother was wicked and brought her own two daughters to live with him. They were beautiful on the outside but ugly within. They took away the girl's clothes and treated her like a despised servant. They made her life miserable and her chores much harder. Because she was always dirty, they called her Aschenputtel, the Little Cinder Girl.

One day, their father went to a market fair and asked his three daughters if they wanted anything. The two stepsisters demanded clothing and jewels, while Aschenputtel only wanted a twig. And so, he brought her back a hazel twig, which she took to her mother's grave and planted. Her tears fell and watered it, and it eventually grew into a tree. She visited it every day, and soon, a white bird appeared and told her that she could make a wish and the bird would grant it for her.

After a time, the king declared a three-day festival and asked all the young ladies of the realm to attend so that his son the prince might meet them and perhaps choose a wife. The stepsisters were delighted, and they insisted that Aschenputtel help them prepare. She wanted to go too and begged her stepmother to let her. But the older woman told her no because she had no dress or shoes. The stepmother then threw lentils into the hearth ashes and told Aschenputtel that if she could pick them

all up in two hours, she could go—an impossible task. Aschenputtel called out to the birds of the garden, asking for their help. Two white doves flew in and picked up the lentils for her in only an hour. Aschenputtel took the dish to her stepmother, who again refused and asked her to pick up more lentils. Aschenputtel called for the doves again, and again they picked out the lentils for her. But as before, the stepmother refused, saying that Aschenputtel had no proper clothes. Then she and her daughters left to go to the celebration on their own.

Aschenputtel went to the tree and made her wish, and the bird gave her a dress of silver and gold, along with beautiful silk slippers. And so, she was able to attend the festival. Once there, her stepmother and stepsisters didn't even recognize her. The prince saw her and was completely enchanted, refusing to dance with anyone else all evening. He wanted to go home with her to see where she lived, but she fled home and hid her dress at her mother's grave. The following night, she went to the festival again, having wished for an even more splendid dress. And again, the prince would dance with no one else. And again, she fled home to put on her dirty dress. And on the third night, the bird gave her a gown and slippers of gold, such that she dazzled at the ball.

But when she tried to run away once more, the prince had devised a plan and had smeared pitch on some of the steps. This caught one of her shoes as she fled. The prince picked it up and took it to his father the king the next morning. The young prince declared that he would only marry the woman on whose foot this slipper fit.

The stepsisters heard of this and wanted to try on the slipper when the prince visited their home, but both had feet that were too large. The first sister cut off a toe to try to fit in, the second sister part of her heel. But they bled as they tried to leave with him, and the prince knew that they could not be the owners of the shoe. "Have you another daughter?" he asked. Aschenputtel's stepmother said, "Only a small one, who couldn't possibly be the one you seek." But the prince ordered them to bring out Aschenputtel to try on the slipper.

Aschenputtel washed her face, went to the prince, and placed her foot into the slipper. It was a perfect fit! He knew at once that this was the beautiful young lady he had danced with each night. He put her on his horse to take her back to the palace. Two pigeons that sat in the hazel tree flew down and landed on her, one on each shoulder.

The young couple were soon wed and the stepsisters came to the wedding, hoping that they might yet gain some favor from the prince and king, even as jealousy burned in them. But the pigeons, seeing the stepsisters' wickedness and deception, flew down to them and picked out their eyes so that they had to live the rest of their miserable days in darkness.

Hansel and Gretel

(Brothers Grimm)

A poor woodcutter and his wife lived near a great forest with their two children—a boy, Hansel, and a girl, Gretel. The family was very poor, and the wife suggested that they abandon the children in the forest to be rid of them and ease their burden. He resisted, but she told him they would all starve if they didn't commit this evil deed. He finally agreed, but he felt much guilt and grief. Unbeknownst to the parents, the children had heard this conversation and wept because they knew their lives were at an end.

But Hansel had an idea and stole some flint stones and put them in his pocket. The next day, their parents took them into the forest while they cut wood, and Hansel left a trail so that he and Gretel could find their way back. Sure enough, their parents tricked them and abandoned them, but the children were able to come home, following the stones. Their father was delighted, but their mother was not. As things grew even more scarce, they took the children again into the forest with them to cut wood, but to a place the children had never been before. This time, Hansel left a trail made with breadcrumbs. Once again, their parents abandoned them, but this time, birds had eaten the crumbs so that the children were lost and couldn't find their way home. They wandered alone and afraid.

On the third morning, a white bird led them along until it perched on a strange house built of gingerbread, with a roof of cake and windows of clear sugar. The hungry children helped themselves to bits of it, and it was delicious. Before too long, an old woman came out, supporting herself with a crutch. "Who is nibbling on my house?" she asked.

The children were afraid, but she invited them inside and fed them milk and pancakes, fruits and nuts. She gave them each a bed to sleep in, and they were delighted at this turn in their fortune.

But this was no kindly old lady; rather, she was a wicked witch who had built this house to entice little children into it. There, she would fatten them up, then kill them and eat them. The next morning, she eyed them as they slept, gloating about what a fine feast they would make. She grabbed Hansel and locked him in a stable and demanded that Gretel fetch water and make food for the boy. Gretel cried bitterly, but she had no choice. Hansel was fed the best of foods, while Gretel got nothing more than scraps and bread crusts.

The witch couldn't see very well and demanded that Hansel show a finger that she might feel it to see if it was fat enough to eat. But Hansel found a small bone to hold out instead. And so he did this for four weeks, and the witch thought that he hadn't grown fat at all. She grew impatient at last and decided to kill him and cook him the next day. Gretel again cried bitterly as she fetched water for his cooking pot.

The witch heated an oven and had prepared some dough to make bread. She pushed Gretel toward it to check on its heat, intending to shove her in and cook her as well. Gretel, realizing the witch's plan, pretended not to know how to check the heat. Grumbling, the witch bent over to show her, and Gretel pushed her in instead and shut the door! The witch screamed as the oven burned her alive.

Gretel ran to Hansel and freed him, and they hugged and rejoiced. Then, they searched the house and found jewels and pearls, which they piled into their pockets and Gretel's apron.

But they still had to escape from the witch's wood. They wandered until they came to a river, but there was no bridge to cross it. A white duck swam by, and they asked if it would carry them across, one at a time, since they were so laden with treasure. The duck happily agreed.

After they had crossed, they continued on until they came to some familiar surroundings. Finally, they saw their house in the distance and ran to it. Their father, hearing them, came out to greet them with hugs and tears. He was so grateful that they had returned. While the children had been gone, his wicked wife had died, and they didn't have to worry about her trying to abandon them anymore. And now that they had the witch's jewels, they never needed to fear going hungry again.

Rapunzel

(Brothers Grimm)

A man and his wife desired a child but had not yet had one. Their small house backed up to a great walled garden, filled with flowers, trees, and vegetables. The garden belonged to a powerful witch, and none dared to enter it, but one day the wife saw some beautiful rampion flower (also known as Rapunzel) from her window, and she thought it would be delicious. She asked her husband to get some for her, for she was soon miserable without it. The desire grew stronger, and her husband finally agreed to climb over the wall at dusk. Once there, he quickly snatched up some rampion and brought it back to her.

She added it to a salad, and it tasted so good that she asked him to go and fetch more despite the danger. Soon, her desire for the rampion was so strong that she fell ill and would die without it. Once again, he climbed the wall to fetch more rampion. But the witch was there waiting for him, glaring at him with angry eyes.

"How dare you sneak into my garden, thief?"

The man begged for mercy, telling her that his wife might have died had he not fetched her the flower. The witch listened and made him an offer. "You may have as much rampion as you like, but I will lay claim to your firstborn child, whom I will care for as if I were its true mother."

The man agreed, happy to have access to the rampion. But as fate would have it, the couple did conceive a child after all. And the witch came to them and demanded the baby after she was born. The witch called the girl Rapunzel, and when she was older, she became the most beautiful child in the world, and her beautiful golden hair had grown to a great length. When Rapunzel was twelve, the witch locked her away in a tall tower in the middle of a forest. It had no door or steps, only a small window at the top. So when the witch wanted to visit her and enter into the tower, she would stand below the window and call up, "Rapunzel, Rapunzel! Let down your hair!" And Rapunzel would let down her hair so that the witch could climb it.

One day some years later, a prince rode by, and he heard Rapunzel singing from the window. He was enchanted by Rapunzel's beautiful song, but he could see no way in—until he witnessed the witch come to the foot of the tower and climb up her hair. He came back at dusk the next day and called out to her, "Rapunzel, Rapunzel! Let down your hair!" And she did, so that he could climb up and see her.

At first, she was terrified, for she had never seen a man before. But he spoke soothing words to her and told her how her singing had won his heart. She was moved and agreed to leave and go with him, but they had no way to escape the tower together. She asked him to bring silk rope each time he visited in the future, and she would fashion a ladder from it. From then on, the two met in secret, the prince visiting her at night, while the witch came during the day. Soon, Rapunzel and the prince fell in love.

But one day, Rapunzel misspoke to the witch, asking why she climbed the tower so slowly, when the prince could climb up it so quickly. The witch flew into a rage, knowing that her attempt to keep Rapunzel hidden from the world had failed. She grabbed Rapunzel by the hair, slapped her many times, and, taking up some shears, cut Rapunzel's beautiful hair off. She then dragged Rapunzel off to a wasteland and left her there alone. Rapunzel lived in misery and sadness for a long time.

The witch went back to the tower and fashioned Rapunzel's hair into a rope of its own. Soon, the prince returned and called out, "Rapunzel, Rapunzel! Let down your hair!"

She let down the hair and the prince climbed up. But he found no trace of Rapunzel, only the evil witch who now glared at him with hatred. "You came for your darling bird," she mocked, "but she is no longer here. A cat has got her, and she no longer sings. You will never see her again!"

The prince threw himself from the window, but he landed in a bramble of thorns that tore out his eyes. He wandered then, miserable and alone, eating berries and lamenting for his lost love. He continued in this terrible state for a few years, until he came at last to the wasteland where the witch had banished Rapunzel. It turned out that she had given birth to twins from their lovemaking, a girl and a boy.

And when she saw him, she drew near and wept, for she recognized him even in his woeful state. She hugged him and cried for joy. Her tears fell into his eyes and cured him of his blindness. Then, he took her and their children and returned to his palace, where they were welcomed with great rejoicing and relief. And there, they married at last and lived long and happily.

Rumpelstiltskin

(Brothers Grimm)

Once there was a poor miller, whose daughter was very beautiful. At one point, the miller happened to meet the king and sought to impress him. "My daughter can spin straw into gold," he declared with pride.

The king was impressed and asked the miller to bring her the next day to the palace so that he might test her. Once there, she was taken by the king to a room filled with straw. "Get you to work," the kind commanded. "Spin for the whole night, and if you have not turned all this straw to gold by morning, you will die." He locked the door to the room and left her alone.

But of course, the poor young lady had no idea of how to spin straw into gold, and so she despaired and began to cry. But before too long, the door opened again, and a small man stood in the doorway. He stepped in and asked her why she was crying.

"I must spin this straw into gold, but I do not know how," she answered tearfully.

"I can do it, but what will you give me?" the little man asked.

"You can have my necklace," she answered.

He took it and sat down to spin, working all night. And by morning, he'd spun all the straw into gold. The king saw the result and was very happy, but he immediately wanted more. He took her to another room, this one even larger, and told her to spin again if she wanted to live. As she despaired, the little man once more appeared and asked what she would give him to do the work for her again.

"My ring," she answered.

He took the ring and set to work, spinning all the straw into gold. And once again, the king was delighted, but being a greedy man, he still wanted more. He took her to still another larger room and told her that if she spun this straw into gold, he would marry her and make her his queen. And once again, the little man came and asked what she would give him to do this work for her.

"I have nothing left," she cried.

"Then give me your firstborn child, after you become queen," he said.

She promised this, and in the morning, when the king found the room again full of gold, he married her and she was crowned queen. About a year later, she gave birth to a child, and one day soon after, the little man appeared and demanded what she had promised. She offered him her wealth instead, but he insisted and would not be deterred.

"No treasure is dearer to me than something living. But I will give you three days," he said. "If you can guess my name in that time, you may keep your child."

She tried to think of every name possible, but with each guess, he simply told her, "That is not my name." And this went on for two more days.

But on the third day, a servant returned and told her that he had found a small house in the woods, and inside, a funny little man danced around a fire, saying that on the morrow, he would take the queen's child, and it was good that she didn't know that his name was Rumpelstiltskin.

And the next day, the little man came once more to her and asked if she knew his name.

"Is it Heinz?" she asked.

"No."

"Is it Kunz?"

"No." He smiled a smug smile.

"Is it... Rumpelstiltskin?"

"Ah!" he wailed. "The devil told you this!" He stomped about so hard that his foot sank into the ground, and he fell in up to his waist. He tried to lift himself out, but taking hold of one foot, he ripped himself in two and died at once.

The Children of Hameln

(Brothers Grimm)

It happened that in the year 1284, a stranger appeared in the German town of Hameln. He wore a coat of many different colored pieces of cloth, and he was called the Pied Piper. He told the town's rulers that he was a rat catcher, and for a price, he could rid them of any rats. Now, Hameln did have a serious problem with rats and mice, so the people made a deal with him. They agreed to pay a certain generous price in exchange for him ridding them of their problem.

So, the piper took up his fife and began to play. As his tune rose over the town, rats and mice began to emerge from houses and many other buildings and follow him. He led them on to the River Weser where, by some miracle, he walked onto the water. But all of the rodents followed him and when they hit the water, they fell in and drowned. And so, the piper got rid of all of Hameln's rats in one fell swoop.

The people were delighted, but seeing how it had not been difficult for him to lure the creatures away, they began to regret offering to pay him so much. And so, they agreed that they would pay him much less. The piper was angry about this, but ultimately, the town refused to pay him at all. He left then, and they were delighted to have had his services without having to give away any money. But they would soon regret their decision.

The piper retuned on June 26—St. John's and St. Paul's Day—early in the morning (though some say it happened at noon). He now wore a hunter's coat and a red hat, and his expression was one of bitterness and anger. He played his fife once more, but this time, the children of Hameln answered his call. They poured forth from their homes and began to follow him, as if in a trance. Nothing the people could do would dissuade their young ones from answering the piper's call. Even the mayor's own daughter joined them. And soon, they followed him out of town.

A young woman happened to see them, and she followed close behind. She saw the piper lead the children into a cave in a nearby mountain, Poppenberg, where he disappeared. She ran back to the town to tell of what she saw, and its citizens at once went in search of the boys and girls. Mothers sobbed and fathers sent out messengers, but to no avail. Only two children managed to escape their fate by turning back. But no one saw the piper or the other children ever again. In all, 130 of them vanished, following his evil lead.

The people put up two stone monuments at Poppenberg, and some say that the cave led from Germany to Transylvania, but that might just be fanciful talk. The town began to date all of its records from the day that the children vanished, so that they would never be forgotten. The officials also minted coins

and had the sad tale depicted on church windows, that they might remember their arrogance and folly, which cost them their beloved children.

The Juniper Tree

(Brothers Grimm)

A wealthy man and his wife had no children, even though they wished very much to have them. In front of their house stood a juniper tree, and one winter's day, the wife stood beneath it peeling an apple with a knife when she cut herself, spilling some drops of blood into the snow. In that moment, she wished again for a child. By a miracle, she became pregnant, and when the nine months had passed, she gave birth to a boy as white as the snow and as red as her blood. She rejoiced and then died. Her grieving husband buried her by the juniper tree and cried bitterly, but after some time, he married another woman.

They had a child of their own, a daughter, but the new wife looked upon the boy of the dead woman with anger and hatred. She shoved him around, slapped him, and gave him no peace. One day, her daughter asked for an apple, and the wife gave her one from a locked box. When the boy came home from school, she offered him one as well, but he noted how angry she looked. Yet he accepted her offer. She opened the box to let him look in and then slammed the lid down on him, cutting off his head.

The stepmother panicked and ran upstairs to get a large scarf. She set the boy's head on his body and tied the scarf around his neck to hide where she'd severed it. She placed the body on a chair and put an apple in his hand. The girl noticed and asked why he didn't answer when she spoke to him. The stepmother told her to ask again and box his ears if he didn't answer.

So, the girl went and asked for his apple. When he didn't answer, she punched his ear and his head fell off. She ran to her mother to tell her what happened. "Be quiet," the woman said, "and tell no one what you did. We'll cook him in a stew." She chopped the boy's body into small pieces and put them into a cooking pot.

The father came home at last, and his wife served him a bowl of the stew. He wanted to know where his son had gone. She lied, telling him, "To his great uncle's. He will stay there a while."

The father thought it odd that his son hadn't said goodbye, but he ate the stew with his son's body in it, even as the girl cried over her half brother. He ate all the stew, and afterward, the girl took a silk scarf and wrapped up her brother's bones. She carried them out to the juniper tree and laid them out beneath it on the green grass. Suddenly, the tree began to move and shake. A mist grew up and a beautiful bird flew out of it. As it flew away, the tree stilled and the boy's bones were gone.

The bird flew to a goldsmith's home and sang of how his mother had killed him, his father ate him, and his sister gathered up the bones and laid them beneath a juniper tree. Giving the bird a gold chain, the smith asked to hear the song again, and so the bird sang. Then the bird flew to a shoemaker's house and sang the same song for an offer of red shoes. His wife, daughter, and apprentices all heard the sad tale. Then the bird flew to a miller's and sang, and when the miller gave him his millstone, the bird sang again.

With these gifts, the bird flew back to the juniper tree and the house. There, the father and daughter were calm enough, but the stepmother was restless and feared something terrible was about to happen. Alighting on the tree, the bird sang its sorrowful song again. The man thought the singing was beautiful and went outside to hear it. The bird dropped the golden chain onto his neck, and it was a perfect fit. The girl went next. The bird dropped the red shoes at her feet, and when she tried them on, they fit so well that she danced for joy.

The stepmother was now very afraid, but she too went outside, and in an instant, the bird dropped the millstone on her head, crushing her skull and killing her at once.

Now, flames and smoke grew up all around, and when they cleared, the bird was gone and the boy reappeared, alive and whole. He came to them and took their hands. And the three went inside and were very happy.

Herr Korbes

(Brothers Grimm)

Once, there was a rooster who wanted to go on a journey, and a hen wanted to go with him. But they would not be walking. Instead, the rooster had a beautiful carriage built, resting on four red wheels. He gathered together four mice and hitched them to it, like horses. The hen was pleased when she saw it and climbed onto it. And so, they set off together. As they went along, they encountered a cat.

"Where are you going?" the cat asked.

"We are going to Herr Korbes's house," the rooster answered.

"Ah, well I would like to come too," the cat answered. "Take me with you."

The rooster was pleased enough with the cat's request. "We'll gladly take you along," said the rooster. "Come aboard but stay in the back so that you won't fall off the front of the carriage. I don't want my fine wheels to get dirty. Be on your way, mice, for we are going to Herr Korbes's house!"

Along the way, they met several more interesting things: a millstone and an egg were next. After that, they met a duck and then a pin and lastly a needle. Each in turn requested to come along on the journey to Herr Korbes, and each climbed aboard the carriage. What a sight they must have been!

They finally arrived at Herr Korbes's house, only to discover that he wasn't there. So, the mice took the carriage into his barn while the hen and the rooster flew up a pole and sat. Meanwhile, the cat went and curled up before the fireplace while the duck found a water bucket and rested inside it. The egg decided to roll itself into a towel and the pin put itself into a chair cushion. The needle went to the bed and rested in the middle of a pillow, while the millstone settled itself down above the front door of the house.

Herr Korbes finally came home. He decided to make a fire, but the cat tossed ashes into his face. He went to get water from the bucket and clean himself, but the duck splashed that water all over his face as well. He tried to use the towel to dry off, but the egg rolled out, broke, and its innards glued his eyes shut. Herr Korbes then tried to sit on the chair, but the pin stuck him. Going to bed, he threw himself onto it, but the needle on the pillow stabbed him so hard that he yelped and jumped up and tried to run out of this very unwelcoming house. But when he reached the front door, the millstone fell on his head and killed him.

Herr Korbes was an evil man, you see, and now all of these animals and items gave him what he deserved.

Frau Trude

(Brothers Grimm)

Once there was a young girl who had very particular ideas of her own and was ill-willed and headstrong. Always, when her parents said anything to her or asked her to complete a task, she would disobey them. So, it seemed certain that something bad would happen to her.

One time, she told her parents about Frau Trude. “One day, I would like to go and visit her home,” the girl said. “Many people have said amazing things about it and that strange and unusual events happen there. I am curious about them and would like to see them for myself.”

But her parents told her that she must never go to Frau Trude. Trude was an evil and wicked old woman, they warned, who did terrible things. They forbade their daughter from going and said that if she did, she would no longer be theirs. Some things just could not be forgiven.

But of course, the girl had no intention of obeying her parents. She was too curious, so she went to Frau Trude’s home, disregarding the warnings and the threats.

Once the young girl arrived, Frau Trude came out to greet her but immediately asked, “Why are you so pale?”

She shook with fear and said, “I saw something that scared me.”

“What was it?” the old woman asked.

“I saw a man all in black on your front steps,” the girl answered, her voice shaking.

"Ah, that was just a charcoal burner," Frau Trude answered with a dismissive wave of her hand.

"But then," the girl said, "I saw a man in green."

"He was but a huntsman," the old woman said.

"But then, I saw a man who was blood-red in color," she said, quivering.

"That was just a butcher," the woman said.

"But then," the girl said, now fully shaking, "I looked through your window, and I'm sure I saw a devil with flames on his head."

"Ah!" Frau Trude said with a laugh. "So, you saw the witch in her true outfit. I have, in honesty, been waiting for you for a long while. Now you can light the way for me!"

And then Frau Trude turned the little girl into a block of wood, threw it into her fireplace, and set it alight. When it was burning strongly, she sat down next to it, enjoying its warmth. "What a bright light it gives!" she said happily.

The Three Army Surgeons

(Brothers Grimm)

Once there were three army surgeons who were quite skilled. One evening while traveling, they came to an inn where they wanted to stay for the night. The innkeeper asked them about their skills and what they could do. The first said he could cut off his own hand and reattach it the next morning. The second said that he could tear out his own heart and put it back in its place the next day. The third claimed he would cut his own eyes out and set them back in their sockets the following morning. The innkeeper was impressed!

They had a special salve that they always kept with them, and they set about doing the bloody deeds, placing the hand, heart, and eyes on a plate. The innkeeper gave it to a servant to set in a cupboard for safekeeping overnight. But she had a lover, a soldier, who came to her asking for some food later that evening. She went to the cupboard to fetch something but left the door open.

Now, while she talked with him, a cat came in and saw the hand, heart, and eyes on the plate. In a moment, he took them up and ran off with them. The girl realized what had happened and despaired, but her lover had a solution.

"I will help you," he said. "There is a thief hanging from the gallows outside. I will cut off his hand." She told him to collect the right hand, which he did and brought it back to her. Then, he found the cat and cut out its eyes and brought them to her. As for the heart, she told him that some pigs had been slaughtered

and he could use one of those. She set each out so that a hand, eyes, and a heart all now rested on the same plate. She shut the cupboard and went to bed.

The next morning, the surgeons came downstairs. The servant brought them the plate and, using the salve, they reattached the missing body parts. The innkeeper was impressed and said he would recommend them to everyone. And so, they went on their way.

But while they traveled, the one with the pig's heart would leave their company and start rooting in the dirt. The second one rubbed his eyes, complaining that he couldn't see as well, and asked his friends to help him not to fall. That evening, they came to another inn, and in the bar, they saw a rich man sitting in one corner, counting his money. The man with the thief's hand wandered over and, distracting the rich man, stole some of his coins. "I couldn't help myself!" he claimed.

Later, as they tried to sleep, the one with the cat's eyes could see very well in the dark. They knew that something was wrong and that they must go back to the previous inn. "The innkeeper must have deceived us," they decided.

When they arrived, they demanded an explanation from the innkeeper. Why did they have a thief's hand, a cat's eyes, and a pig's heart? The innkeeper realized that the servant must be to blame, but she had already run away when she saw them coming. The surgeons demanded money from the innkeeper, or they would set his inn on fire. The innkeeper gave them all he had, and while they were happy with it, they would rather have had their original body parts back.

The Strange Feast

(Brothers Grimm)

Some time ago, a blood sausage invited a liver sausage over to her home to have dinner. The liver sausage was delighted and happily accepted. But as soon as she arrived at the blood sausage's house, she started to notice unusual things: She saw a shovel and broom fighting up and down the stairs, and a monkey wandered about with a cut on its head.

This gave her pause, so she went around to each of the blood sausage's rooms, where she saw other strange and unsettling sights. She came back to the blood sausage and told her what she had seen. But the blood sausage simply waved away her fears, saying it was nothing to be concerned about.

The liver sausage wasn't so sure but decided to stay anyway. Soon, the blood sausage went back into the kitchen to check on the meal.

While the liver sausage waited in the other room, she heard a mysterious voice, at first little more than a whisper. But the words were very clear: "Liver sausage! This is a warning! You are in a dangerous and bloody trap. You need to leave now if you want to live!"

Struck by these words, and still not knowing where they came from, the liver sausage nevertheless jumped up and headed for the door. She heard the blood sausage behind her, yelling and chasing after her. Once outside, the liver sausage dashed into the street and kept on running.

She happened to turn back and saw the blood sausage through the attic window at the top of the house holding a long, sharp knife and waving it about.

The blood sausage shouted to the liver sausage, "If I had been able to catch you, I would have had you!"

The liver sausage knew that she would have been on the dinner menu, a part of a very strange feast indeed. So, she kept on running until she was safely at home, and she never went near the blood sausage's house again.

The Robber Bridegroom

(Brothers Grimm)

There was once a miller who had a beautiful daughter. When she was old enough to be married away, he wanted to make sure that the man who asked her was a suitable match, wealthy, and respectable. Soon, a young man came to him who seemed rich and well positioned, and the miller offered him her hand in marriage, but the daughter didn't like him. Something about him unsettled her, filling her with a sense of horror.

The young man asked her to visit him, saying that his home was in the forest. When she protested that she wouldn't be able to find it, he offered to leave a trail of ash so that she could follow it. He told her that she needed to come next Sunday to a party with other guests. She finally agreed, and when the day came, she followed the ash trail into the woods but scattered her own peas and lentils beside it as she walked.

She found the house at last, but it upset her because it was dark and seemed evil. Before she could enter, a bird in a cage hanging from an outside wall called out to her:

> Turn back, turn back, young bride.
> You are in a murderer's house.

But despite the warning, she entered, and moving from one room to another found the house to be empty; there were no guests, no would-be suitor, not a single human soul. She came to the cellar and saw an old woman sitting near a cauldron of water. She asked the old woman if the man she was meant to marry lived here.

"Oh, my dear," the woman replied. "You will not find marriage here, but death. Those that live in this house are cannibals. They will chop you up and put the pieces in this water to cook. Then they will eat you. But I will help you!"

The woman hid her in a barrel and told her to stay completely quiet. They would make their escape together later that evening.

As they did this, the man and his cronies came home, dragging with them another young lady who screamed and sobbed. Tearing away her clothes, they put her on a table and chopped her to bits, salting the meat afterward. One of these fiends saw a golden ring on the victim's finger and tried to take it off, but when it wouldn't budge, he took an axe and chopped off the whole finger. It flew up through the air and landed in the lap of the miller's daughter, now hiding in the barrel. The old woman distracted them from looking for it and gave them wine containing a sleep-inducing potion. Soon, they had all fallen asleep.

The bride-to-be snuck out of the cellar with the old woman, and they fled from the cannibals' home. Outside, the wind had blown away the ash, but the trail she'd left of peas and lentils remained, and they were able to follow it back to her father's house. She told him what had happened, and he devised a plan to capture these evil men.

The wedding day arrived and the miller invited many guests. They sat at a table and each offered to tell the group something. When the bridegroom-to-be nudged the miller's daughter to get her to speak, she said she would tell them about a dream she'd had. She then relayed the whole story of her finding the house and the horrid crimes she'd seen in it.

"It was only a dream, darling," the evil man said.

But then she told them the part about the finger that had landed in her lap. "And here it is!" she announced, holding up the finger for all to see, the ring still stuck on the knuckle.

With that, her would-be husband jumped up and tried to flee, but other guests caught him and held him down. He was arrested and his whole gang were brought before a court, where they were tried, sentenced, and executed for their horrific crimes.

The Ungrateful Son

(Brothers Grimm)

A man once sat outside with his wife by the front door to their house. The day was nice, and they had a roasted chicken that they intended to eat for their evening meal. But before they could enjoy it, the man spied something: His father was approaching from up the road.

Now, the man really didn't want to have to share the chicken with his father, so instead of being welcoming and offering him a place at their table, he quickly hid the chicken away, so the old man would never even know that they had it. It was a cruel and selfish trick, but the son was determined to keep the roasted fowl only for himself and his wife.

And his plan worked. The father sat with them for a time, had a drink, and then went on his way, unfed.

Satisfied with his deception, the man went to fetch the chicken so that he and his wife could dig in. But as he placed it back on the table, the chicken transformed into a large toad. At once, it jumped onto the greedy son's face and would not move. Nothing he could do would dislodge it. He asked others to try to get it off, but each time one of them tried, the toad glared at them in a threatening manner, and each thought that it might jump onto his face instead. So, no one ever dared try to remove it.

The man had no luck. The toad stayed there for the rest of his life. He had to feed it something every day, or it would start to eat at his face. And ever after, the man had to go about in the world with this giant toad stuck to his face, never free of it, never able to fully rest again—his punishment for being so ungrateful toward his father.

The Goose Girl

(Brothers Grimm)

Once upon a time, there was an old queen whose husband had died many years before. She had a beautiful daughter who was due to marry a handsome prince in a faraway land. When the day came for her to depart, her mother packed up gold, silver, and jewels, all a part of her royal dowry. The princess also possessed a horse named Falada who could talk, and she was to be accompanied by a chambermaid.

Just before the young woman left, the queen took out a small knife and cut her fingers and let three drops of blood fall onto a white cloth, which she then gave to her daughter. "Take care of this cloth and these drops of blood," she said. "They will help you." Her daughter promised she would, and off they rode.

The day was hot, and the princess asked her companion if she would take the princess's cup and fill it with water from the brook. "Get it yourself," the chambermaid said in a haughty tone. "I am not your servant." The princess went to the brook and drank, but she lamented her situation. "If your mother knew this," the drops of blood on the cloth said, "her heart would break."

Later, they stopped again for water, and again the chambermaid refused to serve her. And once more, the drops of blood spoke of the queen's heartbreak. However, as the princess leaned over the water to gather her drink, the cloth fell unseen into the brook and drifted away. By losing it, she lost all of her power and the chambermaid rejoiced.

When the princess went to mount her horse again, the chambermaid spoke up. "I belong on Falada," she sneered. "You

can ride my old nag." And the princess could only obey. The chambermaid ordered her to switch clothing with her and to say nothing when they arrived at the royal court. Falada saw everything that occurred.

They arrived in the neighboring land and the prince lifted the chambermaid off of Falada, thinking she was the princess. When he asked about the girl on the nag—the real princess—the chambermaid told him that she was a servant and to give her some work. The king decided to have her help a boy called Little Conrad to tend the geese. Then the chambermaid demanded that they cut off Falada's head, fearing that the horse would reveal what she was up to.

The princess heard what had been done to Falada and offered to pay the butcher gold if he would nail the horse's head up in the gateway where each morning she passed with the geese. And so he did. And when she walked by the head the next morning, it spoke, saying that her mother's heart would break if only she knew what had happened. Each day, she and Conrad would take the geese out to the field, and he would ask for a strand of her golden hair, but each day, the wind blew his hat away and she would braid her hair before he came back. The boy grew angry about this and decided to tell the king that he wouldn't tend geese with her any longer.

When the king asked why, he explained and said that the horse's head also spoke to her each morning. After the king hid and heard the horse's voice, he called the princess to him and asked her to explain its meaning. She told him that she could not, and so he offered to have her tell her sorrows to a stove. Then she did, revealing all and crying most pitifully, while the king secretly listened in at the other end of the stove pipe. By doing this, he learned that she was the real princess, and not a goose girl at all, and that the chambermaid had deceived them.

The king came back to her and had her dressed in fine clothing, and everyone marveled at the beauty of the true princess. He then summoned his son and told him that he had been deceived by the chambermaid, as had they all. The prince grew angry but was delighted to see that here was his true bride. And so, they threw a party and a grand feast, making sure not to tell the chambermaid what they knew.

The prince sat at the head of the table with the true princess on one side and the chambermaid on the other, though the chambermaid did not recognize the princess, as she was all arrayed in her finery. When they had eaten and drunk their fill, the king posed a question to the chambermaid, asking her what punishment a servant should have for deceiving a king and prince and for harming the good reputation of a princess.

The chambermaid smiled smugly. "She deserves to be stripped naked and sealed into a barrel that is studded inside with sharp nails. Then, two horses should drag the barrel through the streets until such a traitor is dead."

"Ah, you are the one!" the king accused, pointing his finger at her. "You have pronounced your own sentence, and this will be done to you!"

And then, screaming, she was dragged outside, sealed in a barrel with nails, and horses dragged her through streets until she died in a most horrible way. And soon afterward, the prince married the true princess, and together, they ruled the kingdom in peace and happiness.

Fitcher's Bird

(Brothers Grimm)

At one time, there was an evil sorcerer, Fitcher, who disguised himself as a poor man and would go from house to house, begging. At one home, a young woman brought him some bread. But instead of taking the bread, he touched her and she was compelled to jump into his basket. For this sorcerer was also a thief who kidnapped young women. He brought her back to his home, which was decorated in a splendid manner, and he offered her everything she could want.

One day, he said to her, "I must go out and will be away for some time. Here is an egg, which you must take good care of. And here is a key that you must guard, but you must never open the door that it unlocks and go into the room beyond."

She agreed, but as soon as he had left, she went to the door and used the key. In the middle of the room there sat a large basin. She crossed over to it and was horrified to see that it was filled with dismembered dead people and body parts. She screamed and dropped the egg into the basin, getting it coated with blood. She retrieved it but, try as she might, she could not wipe the blood off, for it would reappear the instant that she cleaned the egg.

The sorcerer returned and wanted his egg and key back. When she reluctantly handed them over, he saw that the egg was covered in blood, and he knew.

"You have not heeded my words," he said in an angry voice. "So now, you will go into the room as well!"

He took her by the arm and dragged her into that awful place, where he chopped her into pieces and threw her body parts into the basin.

Soon after, he went out again, disguised as a beggar, and returned to the same house where he had stolen the first young woman. He managed to abduct another daughter and bring her to his home. He gave her the same conditions, but she, too, opened the door, got caught, and was cut up and thrown in the basin.

He returned again and found the third daughter, taking her to his house and giving her the same warning. But this daughter was clever. She put the egg in a safe place before going into the forbidden room. Inside the basin, she found her sisters' body parts and began to piece them together. And as she did so, they both came back to life! She snuck them out of that terrible room and hid them away in a closet.

The sorcerer returned and found that the egg was blood-free, so he asked the third sister to marry him at once. She consented, but he would have to pay her parents a handsome sum of gold as a dowry and carry it in a basket back to them. She told him that he must not stop on the way back to her home, for she would be able to see him the whole time. He agreed, but he didn't know that she'd hidden her sisters in the basket and covered them with gold, instructing them to call for help to put an end to this madman's evil.

With the golden girls inside, the basket was unbearably heavy. The sorcerer struggled to carry the basket and more than once wanted to stop and rest, but each time he tried, one of the sisters would call out, "I can see you from my window. Stop resting and walk at once!"

Meanwhile, the third daughter dressed up a skull and put it in the attic window. She then smeared herself in honey, cut open the bed, and rolled herself in feathers to hide her identity.

She left the house and soon met some of the guests who were coming to the wedding.

"Where are you coming from, Fitcher's Bird?" one asked.

"I am coming from Fitcher's house," she answered.

"And where is his young bride?"

"She is cleaning the house and is in the attic even now."

The sorcerer then returned from delivering the gold and, unknowingly, the sisters. He asked Fitcher's Bird (the young lady) the same questions the guests had, and she told him that his bride-to-be was in the attic. The sorcerer saw the decorated skull in the window, waved at it, and went inside his house, thinking it was his bride-to-be. He then invited his guests in for a wedding party.

But soon the others came, those who'd been sent by the sisters. While the daughter in her bird disguise watched, they barricaded the house and set it on fire. Unable to escape, the wicked sorcerer and his guests all died, burned by the flames.

How Some Children Played at Slaughtering

(Brothers Grimm)

Version 1:

Once in a city in West Friesland, three boys and two girls were playing, when they decided to play butcher. One boy would play the butcher, while another would be the cook, and the third, the smallest, would take the role of the pig to be slaughtered. The girls would pretend to be a cook and an assistant who would help to catch the blood of the "pig" as it spilled out. That way, they could make blood sausages.

But as they began to play, the "butcher" boy threw the "pig" boy to the ground and, taking up a knife, slit his throat for real. The assistant girl then caught his blood in a bowl. A councilman happened to walk by and saw this grisly event. He grabbed the butcher boy by the collar and dragged him off to the mayor's house, where the council met in private and debated what to do with him.

One councilman suggested that they offer the boy the choice between a red apple and a gold coin. If the boy chose the apple, they would let him go free, but if he took the coin, they would execute him at once. And so, they presented the boy with the choice, but he chose the apple, laughing as he did so, and they had no other option but to set him free.

Version 2:

Once, a father went about the business of slaughtering a pig. His young sons saw him and decided to play at it themselves. So, after he had gone off to work in the fields, the older brother said to the younger, "You shall be the pig, and I the butcher."

Then, he took a knife and slit his brother's throat.

Now, their mother was upstairs bathing the third son (who was very young) when she heard the boy's cries. She ran down to see what had happened, and she was so upset at the bloody sight that she grabbed the knife from the boy butcher's hand and stabbed him in the throat. She quickly ran back upstairs to look in on her third child, but while she was gone, he had accidentally drowned in the bathtub.

The mother was so distraught that all of her sons were dead that she hanged herself in grief. Her husband returned home later that day from his field work, and when he saw what had happened, he became so despondent and overcome that he, too, died soon after.

Mother Holle

(Brothers Grimm)

Once upon a time, there was a girl who lived with her terrible stepmother and stepsister. The stepmother hated the girl, and the stepsister was so lazy that she couldn't be bothered to do much of anything. Yet the stepmother would also blame the girl for her stepsister's wrongdoings. So, one day, the stepmother decided to be rid of the girl altogether. She dragged her out to a well and threw her in, hoping that she would drown.

But something strange and even miraculous happened instead. The girl woke up, not at the bottom of the well but in a lovely new land that she didn't know. Nor did she have any idea how she'd come to be there. She got up and began walking to see what wonders this place might hold. She happened to come to a house with several chores in need of doing: apples that needed picking from a tree outside, bread that should be baked, and the house itself in need of cleaning. So, she resolved to do each of the tasks.

When she'd finished, a wizened old woman, Mother Holle, returned. Impressed by what she saw, she made the girl an offer. "Be my servant for a year, and I shall reward you handsomely."

Having no other choice in this new place, the girl accepted and worked hard throughout the year, doing everything that Mother Holle requested and required. And at the end of that year, the old woman was true to her word and gave the girl gold and jewels.

The girl decided to return to her stepmother, hoping that her changed circumstances would make things better between them. The stepmother was delighted with the newfound wealth, but before the girl could even finish the whole story of how she attained it, the stepmother dragged her own daughter to the well and pushed her in, hoping that she would return in a year with even more gold.

The stepsister found herself in the same land as the girl and soon made her way to Mother Holle. But she was lazy and disobedient. She demanded of Mother Holle that she be made a servant so that she too could be showered in riches. Yet she picked no apples, baked no bread, and cleaned nothing. So, Mother Holle dismissed her after a few days.

Still, the stepsister demanded some kind of reward. Instead of gold, Mother Holle covered her in pitch and sent her away. When she arrived back home and tried to tell her own story, snakes and toads began to wriggle out of her mouth. One giant toad leapt onto the stepmother's face and began to chew on her nose. And it has remained on her nose ever since.

The Girl Without Hands

(Brothers Grimm)

A poor miller had almost nothing to his name except his mill and an apple tree. Once, he went into the forest to gather some wood. An old man met him there and offered to make him wealthy if he would sign over that which stood by the mill. The miller thought he meant the apple tree, and readily agreed.

"I will return for my prize in three years," said the old man.

When the miller returned home, his wife was astonished and demanded to know why so much wealth had appeared suddenly in their humble home. He explained his deal, but his wife was horrified. "That was the devil!" she said. "Our daughter was behind the home earlier, doing chores!"

Three years later, their daughter had grown into a beautiful young woman, but knowing what would happen, she washed her hands and drew chalk around herself in a circle. And the devil could not take her, so he grew angry. "Keep water away from her," he told the miller, "so that she cannot be clean, and then I can have power over her."

The miller, now frightened, did as the devil asked, but the next day, his daughter had wept into her palms, again fully cleaning them. The devil was furious and ordered the miller to chop off her hands. The father was horrified and refused, but the devil said he would take the miller instead if he chose not to listen. So, the miller went to his daughter and begged her forgiveness, and then chopped her hands off. When the devil came again, she had wept for so long into the stumps that they were again clean, and he could not take her.

The miller was now wealthy and said that he would care for her forever, but she resolved to leave her home. Tying her chopped-off hands to her back, she set off. Soon, she found the king's garden. Sneaking in, she shook an apple tree with her arms, and when the fruit fell to the ground, she picked them up with her teeth to eat them. Soon, guards caught her and threw her in prison. The king wanted to banish her, but his son asked if she could tend the chickens instead. The king agreed and the prince visited her often and he became fond of her.

The king decided that the prince should soon marry, and the prince asked to marry the chicken minder with no hands. The king was shocked but eventually agreed. Not long after, the king died, and his son succeeded him. Later, this new young king went off to war and his handless bride gave birth to a child.

She sent out a messenger to tell him the good news, but the devil, still trying to cause harm, switched out her letter with one claiming she had given birth to a changeling. The king was sorry for this but sent a message back saying that the child would be cared for in any case.

The devil intercepted the king's message and changed it to one banishing her and her infant from the realm. With no other choice, she once more had her hands tied to her back and set off with the child. In a forest, she met an old man by a spring. He told her to wrap her arms around a nearby tree three times. She did this, and miraculously, her hands grew back! He then offered to let her stay at his house but warned her not to go outside and not to answer the door unless the caller asked three times.

The king had returned home and found out that his wife had been deceived and was gone, so he resolved to set out with a servant looking for her at once. He eventually came to the same forest where she now lived. They found the old man's house, and when the servant looked in the window, he declared that it must be the king's wife, for she looked exactly the same, except that she had hands.

The king went to the door and knocked, asking to be let in. She refused, so he asked again, and again. Upon the third request, she opened the door and saw that it was her husband. He rejoiced in finding her, and after she had told him all that happened, they returned the next morning to his kingdom.

Once they left the house, it vanished before their eyes, and they never had trouble with the devil again.

The Little Mermaid

(Hans Christian Andersen)

A mermaid lived with her family in the underwater realm of her father, the Sea King. But she wanted to know all about the surface world and desired to explore it. She even asked her grandmother to tell her stories about that mysterious land. On her fifteenth birthday, her father let her swim to the ocean's surface to take a look at dry land. Her older sisters each had a chance to go to the surface and live there for one year, but each came back disillusioned and happy to remain underwater.

But the Little Mermaid was enthralled by their stories, and when it was her turn, she went to the surface and saw a prince's birthday party on a ship. She fell in love with him at once, but soon a storm blew in and sank the ship. She saved the prince from drowning and took him ashore near a temple. The temple attendants took him in, but sadly, he never knew that a mermaid had rescued him.

Later, she asked her grandmother about humans. Her grandmother told her that humans have short lifespans compared to mermaids. But when humans died, they lived on forever in heaven, unlike mermaids, who have no souls. When mermaids died, they returned to sea foam and were lost forever. She loved the prince and wanted to obtain a soul for herself, so she went to visit the Sea Witch, whose lair was surrounded by whirlpools and other dangers. The Witch offered the Little Mermaid a potion that would give her legs, but the cost would be her tongue and her beautiful singing voice. And once she became human, the witch warned, she could never come back to the sea.

Furthermore, she would be able to dance beautifully, but it would always feel like she was walking on knives, and her feet would hurt and bleed. Finally, she would not gain a soul unless she could win the prince's love and marry him, for a portion of his soul would become hers. But if he were ever to wed another, she would die of a broken heart and dissolve into sea foam.

She agreed to these terrible terms and swam to the surface, where she took the potion. She did indeed grow legs, which hurt terribly, and the prince found her naked on the shore. The prince was taken with her, but not in a loving way. He kept her nearby, but because she could no longer talk (only dance), he saw her more like a pet than a beloved; she even had to sleep on the floor outside of his bedroom. And yet, though she was in pain (in her feet and her heart), she was happy being able to see so much of the world that she had wondered about. Still, she would go to the seashore each night and bathe her aching feet in the cool ocean water. Her sisters and father and grandmother would come there to visit her, even though they were heartbroken at her decision.

The prince's parents told him he must marry a princess in a nearby land, but he refused, saying he would only marry the woman who rescued him from the sea at the temple. Happily, his parents explained that the maiden who had saved him was indeed the princess herself who had been sent there for her education. And so, he soon celebrated his marriage to her, and the Little Mermaid's heart broke.

She expected to dissolve into nothingness, but her sisters came to her at dawn and offered her a dagger given to them by the Sea Witch in exchange for their long hair. If the Little Mermaid would kill the prince and let his blood flow onto her feet, she would become a mermaid again and live out her life with her family in the sea. But even though he broke her heart, she could not bear to kill him as he slept peacefully with his new bride, and at dawn, she threw herself off the ship and into the water.

Her body began to dissolve into foam, but she transformed into a pure spirit and could speak once more. Other sea daughters came to her and told her that she had become like them, since she sought a soul. Because of this, she was given the chance to do good deeds, and when her time had come, she would die and gain a true soul and be taken into heaven.

The Red Shoes

(Hans Christian Andersen)

A peasant girl named Karen was adopted by a wealthy elderly woman who raised her in privilege and spoiled her. Karen had once owned a pair of old, worn-out red shoes, and she convinced her adoptive mother to buy a fancy new pair of red shoes for her, which she adored. She wanted to wear them everywhere, including to church, which was a completely inappropriate place to have them on. Only black shoes were suitable for church. Though her mother told her not to, she wore them to the services more than once.

At church one Sunday, an old soldier saw them and said, "What beautiful dancing shoes! Never come off when dancing." And at that, a curse descended on Karen, and she felt compelled to start dancing. She even had to be forced into her coach to go home because she couldn't stop.

She was finally able to take them off, but not before kicking her mother. She put them away but still remained obsessed with them. Soon, her mother fell ill and died. Karen should have attended her funeral but opted instead to go to a ball and wear her red shoes. And once again, the shoes took on a life of their

own and she was compelled to dance as they willed. And once again, she saw the old soldier who simply said, "What beautiful dancing shoes!"

Karen was desperate to be rid of them, but they had grown together with her feet and could not be removed. All she could do, day or night, was dance. At one point, she found herself in a graveyard where she met an angel carrying a sword. She begged for help, but the angel offered none, saying instead, "You shall dance in these shoes until you are cold and pale, until your skin shrivels and you are nothing but a skeleton! You will dance from door to door, and wicked children will see you and fear you."

Unable to stop dancing, she took herself to an executioner's house on a moor and begged for him to cut off her feet. He took up his axe and chopped off her feet, but the shoes would not cease their awful dance. They simply danced away, taking her severed feet with them. The executioner made wooden feet for Karen, along with some crutches to help her walk. She resolved to go to church to show that she had changed, but each time she tried, the red shoes, with her feet still in them, would block her from entering.

She feared going to church at all after that, and instead, she prayed for deliverance from her cruel fate. The same angel appeared to her, now holding roses instead of a sword.
He brought her into the church, and she was so filled with peace at last that her heart burst and she died. Her soul flew up to heaven and no one ever mentioned those terrible red shoes again.

The Story of the Thumb Sucker

(Heinrich Hoffmann, *Der Struwwelpeter*, 1845)

Once there was a boy named Conrad who had a habit of sucking his thumbs. Seeing this, his mother became more and more concerned. One day, she said to him, "Dearest Conrad, I have to go out for a while and leave you alone, but please listen to me: Do not suck your thumb while I'm gone."

"Why not?" Conrad asked, about to put his thumb in his mouth.

"Because there is a tall tailor who will come by. He finds little boys who suck their thumbs, and before they can guess what he is doing, he will take out his sharp scissors and cut off those thumbs. And you must know, if he cuts them from you, they will never grow back."

She left him then, but no sooner was she gone than he had put his thumb back into his mouth. Oh, alas! Why did he do that?

Just then, the front door flew open, and there stood the tailor, menacing in his long red pants. He stormed into the house, this tailor, for he had come to cut off the thumbs of Conrad, our little Suck-a-Thumb!

With a snip and a snap, his scissors struck, taking off one of Conrad's thumbs. Conrad cried out, but before he could run, the scissors went snip and snap again, and they took his other thumb! And then the tailor was gone, leaving Conrad alone and bloody without his thumbs.

Soon, his mother returned, and Conrad stood before her, tearful and looking quite sad. He finally held out his bleeding hands and showed her what the evil tailor had done.

His mother took a look at one hand and then the next.

"Ah," she said, without any pity. "I told you what would happen, and since you didn't listen, I knew he would come to you, naughty little Suck-a-Thumb!"

The Very Sad Tale with the Matches

(Heinrich Hoffmann, *Der Struwwelpeter*, 1845)

It might just make you cry to hear the terrible story of young Harriet. One day, her mother and nurse went out and left her all alone to play by herself. On the nearby table, she saw a box of matches. Now, her mother and nurse had both told her not to touch the matches, or they would punish her. They knew how dangerous matches could be.

But Harriet loved how the matches looked when they burned. "The flames are very pretty," she said, "and I love the crackle they make, as does mother."

Her cats heard her talking and started to hiss. They stretched and lifted up their paws. "Meow," they said. "If you light those, you will burn to death."

But Harriet would not heed their advice, and she lit a match. It was beautiful and crackled, just as she'd hoped. She jumped up in excitement and ran around as she held it in her hand, being too excited and pleased with herself to put it out.

The cats saw what she did and again became very concerned. "Naughty child!" they scolded. They stretched and raised their paws again. "This is a very wrong thing that you do, little one. Meow! If you keep doing this, you will burn to death!"

And sure enough, they spoke truly. The flame from that match caught on her apron string and it began to burn. And then the flame spread to her apron, and then to her sleeves and arms, and then to her hair, until she was burning all over.

The cats meowed, but what could they do? They meowed and yowled and screamed for help, but it was no good. No one else could hear them. "What can we do? We told her not to do it, and now she is burning!"

And so, Harriet burned up. Her clothes, arms, hands, eyes, and nose went up in flames, until she had been completely consumed, except for her scarlet red shoes. There was nothing else left except a pile of ashes on the floor.

The good cats came up to the smoking ashes, and they meowed and wailed and cried.

"Meow! Meow!" they lamented. "Now what will Mamma and Nurse do?"

And as they wailed, tears fell from their eyes and made a little pond in the ashes, but they were too late to save Harriet from her terrible fate.

The Flea

(Giambattista Basile, the *Pentamerone*, 1634)

Once there was a king with an unusual hobby. He kept a flea in a bottle and raised it. But it grew and grew, until it could no longer fit in the bottle. Eventually, it became the size of a sheep. But the king wasn't interested in keeping the creature as a giant pet. Instead, he had it killed and skinned. He then promised his daughter's hand in marriage to anyone who could guess where the strange pelt came from. Suitors arrived from all over the land. One guessed it was an ape, another that it came from a crocodile. But all of them were wrong.

Finally, one day, an ugly ogre came to the king. He examined the skin and said that it belonged to the king of the fleas. The king had no choice but to offer his daughter, Porziella, to the ogre. He tried to encourage her that she might yet be happy. When she resisted, he angrily told her to go. And so, the ogre took Porziella to his home in the forest, a ghastly place made from the bones of the people he had eaten.

Soon, the ogre went away and came back with some meat for her to cook. But it was meat from men he had killed. Porziella was repulsed and would not cook or eat it. The ogre told her that he was due to go on a wild boar hunt the following day and would bring back enough for a feast for both of them.

While he was away, she happened to meet an old woman and told her of her plight. The old woman took pity on her and told her that she had seven sons: Mase, Nardo, Cola, Micco, Petrullo, Ascaddeo, and Ceccone. All of them were giants, and each had a special talent that could help her. The old

woman departed and came back the next day, accompanied by her sons. And so, taking Porziella with them, they set off to the king's palace.

The ogre came home and, finding that Porziella was gone, immediately started off after her. But Mase used his fine hearing to warn them that the ogre pursued them. Nardo rubbed his hands and made a mound of soap suds to block the ogre's path, but the ogre ran home and came back with a sack of bran to get past the bubbles without slipping. Then Cola threw a piece of iron to the ground, causing a field of razors to arise. Again, the ogre ran home and came back in iron armor to step over them.

Micco then hit the ground with a stick, and new trees sprang up to make the path impassable, but the ogre drew his fine knife and began to cut them down. Next, Petrullo sprinkled some water on the ground, creating a great river. But the ogre cast off his armor and swam across it. Ascaddeo tossed a pebble to the ground, and up from it sprang a great stone tower into which they all ran. Once again, the ogre went home and came back with a ladder that he set against the tower and began to climb.

Ceccone stepped forward and took aim, tossing an iron ball, which hit the ogre in the head, taking out one of his eyes. The ogre dropped like a fruit from a tree. Then Ceccone went out and cut off the ogre's head as if it were nothing more than soft cheese.

They all then returned to the king, who by now deeply repented his cruelty in forcing his daughter to go with the ogre. Porziella was soon able to marry a prince whom she loved, and the woman and her giant sons were rewarded handsomely for saving her.

Penta of the Chopped-Off Hands

(Giambattista Basile, the *Pentamerone,* 1634)

Once upon a time, there was a young king who loved his wife, but she fell ill and died. The grief he felt made him begin to act without reason or morals, and soon he desired his own sister, Penta. He especially admired her hands. He then begged her to marry him, but of course, she was repulsed and refused. Still, he persisted and would not let her be, always leering at her hands. Penta decided to trick a servant into chopping off her hands, and after her brother discovered what she had done, he was enraged. He locked her in a chest and had it cast out to sea.

Some time later, a fisherman caught the chest and, seeing who was inside, brought Penta to his home. But the fisherman's wife was jealous of such a beautiful young woman (even without hands) and threw her back into the ocean.

Now, the king of another land called Terraverde saw the chest at sea and rescued Penta. He decided to make her the queen's lady-in-waiting. Soon, however, that queen took ill, and as she lay dying, she asked Penta to marry her husband. Penta agreed and she and the king lived happily for some time. But all too soon, he had to go away on official business, and while he was gone, she gave birth. His servants sent a message to the king, but the ship ran aground during a storm and landed near the home of the fisherman who'd rescued her before. The wife, still jealous of Penta, changed the message to read that Penta had given birth to a puppy.

The king received this altered message and declared that it must be the will of fate and that Penta should not worry, for he still loved her. But again, the fisherman's wife intervened and change the letter to demand that Penta and the baby be burned. Now, upon reading this, the king's councilors decided that he must have gone mad, so they banished Penta and the child instead of killing them.

Penta left and journeyed to a land ruled by a wizard. He gave her a place to live and offered to reward whoever could tell him the worst and most miserable story.

Her husband the king returned home at last and learned all that had happened. He realized that his message must have been altered and uncovered that the fisherman's wife had done the deed, so he went to her home and ordered her to be burned. Then, he traveled to the wizard's realm, having heard of his offer. Penta's brother, who had desired her but now deeply regretted his actions, also went. He told the wizard of his wicked deeds, and then Penta's husband told his tale.

The wizard brought out Penta and her child to show that they were both well, and he declared that her husband's story was the most miserable. He then decided that they would be his heirs, and thus Penta and her husband were reunited to live happily together.

Little Red Riding Hood

(Charles Perrault, *Histoires ou contes du temps passé*, 1697)

Once, there was a pretty girl who was well loved, especially by her mother and grandmother. The grandmother was so fond of her that she made a hooded red cloak that fit the girl so well that she became known by all as Little Red Riding Hood. She would go out and about in her cloak and everyone admired it and her.

It happened that her mother once made some cakes and told Red Riding Hood, "Your grandmother has been quite ill, my dear. Take a cake and a pot of butter to her and see how she is doing."

Little Red Riding Hood obeyed her mother and set off at once to see her grandmother, who lived in another village. But to get there, she needed to pass through a forest. As she made her way, she met Gaffer Wolf, who saw her to be a tasty treat. He desired to eat her right then and there, but he could not because there were some stick gatherers nearby, and he was afraid she might call out to them.

So instead he said, "Hello, little child! Where are you going this day?"

Now, Red Riding Hood did not know it was dangerous to speak to wolves, so she answered, "I am off to see my grandmother and take her a cake and a pot of butter, sent from my mother."

"Ah," said Gaffer Wolf, "does she live far away?"

"Indeed," she said. "Her house is beyond the mill there and is the first house in the village."

“Well, then,” the sly old wolf said, “I will go to visit her as well. You go this way, and I shall go another, and we can see who will get there sooner.”

The wolf took off in a run, while Red Riding Hood went on her normal route. She gathered some nuts, chased after butterflies, picked flowers, and generally took her time.

The wolf arrived at the grandmother’s much more quickly and knocked on her door.

“Who’s there?” the grandmother asked.

“It is your granddaughter, Little Red Riding Hood,” the wolf answered, imitating Red Riding Hood’s voice. “I have brought you a cake and a pot of butter from my mother.”

The grandmother, being in bed, said, “Pull on the latch, and the bolt will fall down.”

Gaffer Wolf did as she instructed and the door opened. He at once attacked her and ate her up, for he had eaten nothing for three days. Afterward, he shut the front door and waited. Soon, Little Red Riding Hood knocked on the door.

“Who is there?” the wolf asked.

“It is your granddaughter, Little Red Riding Hood, and I have brought you a cake and a pot of butter from my mother.”

The wolf bade her to come in, so she did. He had hidden himself in the grandmother’s bed and he asked her to set aside her gifts and come near. She took off her cloak and lay down in the bed beside him.

Seeing the wolf in nightclothes, but thinking he was her grandmother, Red Riding Hood said, “What great arms you have!”

“The better to hug you,” Gaffer Wolf replied.

"And what great legs you have!"

"The better to run."

"And grandmother, what great ears you have!"

"The better to hear you, child."

"And what great eyes!"

"The better to see you."

"And grandmother, what great teeth you have!"

"That is so I might eat you!"

And saying that, the wolf attacked and greedily devoured her.

Blue Beard

(Charles Perrault, *Histoires ou contes du temps passé*, 1697)

There was once a rich man who had great wealth and fine houses, but his beard was blue and he was ugly. He had already been married several times before, but no one knew what had become of those wives. Still, he desired a new wife, yet no woman would have him. But through trickery, he was able to convince the youngest daughter of one of his neighbors to marry him after inviting them to grand parties at his estate.

About a month after they were wed, Blue Beard told her that he was going away. He said to do whatever she pleased and gave her the keys to two wardrobes and to all of his gold and silver, jewels, and apartments. He also gave her a small key to a closet at the end of the great gallery.

"Open all of them as you please, save for that little closet," he instructed. "There will be no end to my anger if you go in there."

She promised to heed his request. After he left, she invited friends and family to spend time in his luxurious home. They reveled in this grand place, but she was most curious about the closet that he had forbidden her to open. Though she wavered when she got to it, curiosity got the better of her. She took out the small key, opened the closet door, and stepped in. It was so dark that at first, she couldn't see a thing.

But as she stepped forward, she felt clotted blood on the floor beneath her feet, and she was able to see the bodies of other women hanging on the walls. Now she knew. These were

the other women he had married in the past. Frightened, she dropped the key, but coming to her senses, she picked it up and retreated, locking the closet door behind her.

She saw that the key was stained in blood, but no matter how much she washed it, the blood would not come off. It was an enchanted key and could not be made clean.

Soon, Blue Beard arrived back home from his journey, and the next day, he asked her to return his keys. She did so, her hand trembling, but did not give him the closet key.

"Isn't my closet key here as well?" he asked.

"It must be," she answered with a quavering voice.

But he would not believe her and commanded that she bring the key to him. Eventually, she had no choice.

When he saw it, he asked, "Why is there blood on the key?"

"I know not!" she insisted, growing pale and afraid.

"You have gone into the closet, have you not?" he demanded of her. "Very well, you shall take your place among the ladies inside! You will die, Madame!"

"Then give me time to pray," she begged.

He gave her less than a quarter of an hour. So, she ran to find her sister and begged her to go and keep a lookout for their brothers, who had promised to come visit this day. The sister did, but she did not see them.

Blue Beard took up his scimitar and yelled out to his wife. He told her to come down that instant, but she begged for a moment longer. And still, her sister didn't see their brothers. Blue Beard again threatened her. And again she called to her sister, who saw at last the cloud of dust that indicated riders were on their way.

Blue Beard shouted for her again, and this time she came, throwing herself at his feet to beg for mercy.

"Nothing will avail you," he said, taking her by her hair. "You will die!"

He raised his sword to chop off her head, but at that moment, there was a knocking at the gate and two horsemen entered, a dragoon and a musketeer. Seeing their sister in distress, the two young men rushed for this evil man. Blue Beard ran away, trying to save himself, but before he got far, the brothers caught up with him and ran him through with their swords. Their poor sister was nearly dead herself, so overcome was she by the ordeal.

But since Blue Beard had no heirs, she became lady of his estates and his wealth passed to her. She secured a marriage for her sister and commissions for her brothers and married a kindly gentleman who made her forget all about the vile, murderous Blue Beard.

Donkeyskin

(Charles Perrault, *Histoires ou contes du temps passé*, 1697)

Long ago, there was a king who was lucky enough to have plenty of wealth and a beautiful wife and daughter. Even better, he had a prized donkey who could poop gold, the source of his riches. All was well until one day, the queen took ill and died shortly afterward. Before she died, she made him promise that he would not marry again until he had found a woman who was equal to her. He swore this and mourned her greatly after her passing. And for a long time, he remained alone, until he decided that the only one equal to his wife was his daughter.

Of course, the daughter was disgusted, and she went to her fairy godmother, the lilac fairy, for help. The lilac fairy counseled her to make impossible demands of her father before she would ever consent. She should ask for dresses as bright as the sun, as luminous as the moon, and containing all the colors in the world. But most of all, she should ask the king for the hide of his donkey, the source of all his wealth.

Confident that he could not satisfy her requests, she was astonished and horrified when he brought her all the magnificent dresses as well as the donkey's hide. Since she had no choice now, the fairy told her to flee in the night and to wear the hide as a disguise.

So the princess disappeared, wearing the hide, and came to another kingdom where she took work on a farm. She looked horrible, messy, and dirty in her hide, and those around her nicknamed her "Donkeyskin." But when she spent time in her

room, she would dress in the magnificent multi-colored dresses, in contrast to the roughness of the dirty animal hide.

It happened one day that the prince of this kingdom came by the farm and happened to spy her through her keyhole in one of these beautiful dresses. He fell in love with her at that very moment and declared that nothing could cure him of his sickness, save a cake baked by Donkeyskin.

She agreed to make the cake for him, but while doing so, her ring fell into the batter. Finding it in his slice of cake, the prince declared that he would only marry the woman on whose finger the ring would fit. Women from all over the kingdom tried the ring, but none fit it properly.

Finally, Donkeyskin came forth, wearing the animal's hide once more. The ring slid onto her finger perfectly. She removed the hide to reveal a beautiful dress underneath. Then, the lilac fairy appeared and told the whole sorry story to the king and queen, the prince's parents. They were delighted with her royal heritage and consented to the marriage.

She and the prince were married in a grand ceremony, and Donkeyskin's father attended, though by then, he had found another woman (a widow) to marry and had repented his revolting and sinful desires.

The Crucifix Priest

(Medieval French *fabliaux*)

There was once a wood-carver named Roger, and he made crucifixes and statues for the church. His was a good business, and he was quite skilled in his work. He was married, but his wife was unsatisfied with him. At some point, she decided to begin an affair with a priest, Father Constanz. Roger suspected that something was happening, but he didn't have proof until he returned home early one night and spied them through the window dining together. Roger knew that after the meal, they undoubtedly would go to the bedroom to continue their affair.

Being mischievous, he decided to make some noise to give them warning and to see how his unfaithful wife would react. And sure enough, the wife told the priest to go and hide in Roger's workshop, take off his clothes, and pretend to be a crucifix statue.

Roger came in and sat down with his wife, enjoying the rest of the meal that Father Constanz had been eating. Afterward, he complimented her on the fine food and told her he was going to his workshop for a while. He knew what the two of them had planned, so he asked his wife to come with him and to bring a candle. She had no choice but to agree, lest she look suspicious and risk giving away her secret.

Once in the workshop, Roger stepped up to the naked priest whose arms were stretched out on a wooden cross. "Ah," he said, "I have made a terrible and sinful mistake! Look wife, I have carved private parts on this image when I should not have done so. Here, let me correct that."

He took a sharp knife and cut off the man's private parts, all of them. At that, Father Constanz leapt up, yowled in pain, and ran out of the workshop in a desperate attempt to escape. But Roger would not let him flee. He chased after the priest, shouting to the whole town that his crucifix was escaping. A townsman heard the racket and, seeing the priest, struck him, causing him to fall into the mud.

Roger grabbed hold of Father Constanz and dragged him back to the workshop. There, he told the trembling priest that he knew all about the affair, and he demanded that Constanz pay a hefty sum of money to be let go. The priest, humbled and humiliated, agreed. Roger also kept his "three hanging ornaments" as part of the payment. And any clergyman who would have an affair with a married woman should face the same punishment!

The Story of the Three Bears

(Robert Southey, 1839)

Once, three bears dwelled in a fine house in the middle of the woods. They were quite comfortable and would often go out for walks, after which they would return and eat, smoke, and talk with each other. One bear was large, another of medium size, and the third was quite small.

They would eat their porridge from pots: a large one for the biggest bear, a middle-size one for the next bear, and a small pot for the littlest bear. They each had a chair as well, one each

befitting their sizes. And of course, each had their own bed, which matched their sizes very well.

One morning, as they served their porridge, they found that it was far too hot, and having burned their tongues on hot porridge before, they decided to go for a pleasant walk in the woods and let it cool for a bit.

It happened that while they were gone, an old woman by the name of Silverlocks was wandering in the woods and came upon the bears' house. Curious, she looked through the window and the keyhole, and then lifted the latch to the front door. Finding it unlocked, she crept inside.

She found the porridge pots and decided to sample them. The bears were kind, and if she had just waited until they came home, they might have shared some with her. But she was greedy and helped herself. She tried the porridge from the largest pot, but it was far too hot and she swore and spat it out. The porridge in the second was too cold and not to her liking. But the porridge in the smallest pot was just right, so she ate it all.

She next went to their chairs and found that the largest chair was too hard, while the middle chair was too soft, but the smallest of the three was just right. And so, she stayed there for some time and began to nod off, but her weight was too much for the chair and it broke underneath her. She swore and went upstairs. Finding the three beds, the first two were not to her liking, but the smallest felt just right. Thus, she lay down in it and fell asleep.

A short time passed, and the three bears came home to find their door open. Going to the table, they saw their porridge pots. "Somebody at my porridge pot has been!" shouted the largest bear. The medium bear did the same. The little bear whispered the same and saw that the porridge was all gone. They went to their chairs. "Somebody in my chair has sat!"

The great bear proclaimed, as did the middle bear, while the smallest said the same but saw that the chair was broken.

Going upstairs, they saw that their beds had been disturbed. “Someone’s been lying in my bed!” yelled the big bear, while the next one yelled the same. “Someone’s been lying in my bed,” the littlest declared, “and here she’s lying still!”

They drew close and saw the old woman, slumbering away. Hearing them approach, she awoke and shrieked to see three bears glaring at her. She then ran to the window and jumped out. She fell to the ground, broke her neck, and died.

Vasilisa and Baba Yaga

(Russian fairy tale)

A wealthy merchant and his wife had a daughter, whom others called Vasilisa the Beautiful. When Vasilisa was just eight years old, her mother died, but before she passed away, she gave her daughter a Motanka doll, a kind of talisman. Her mother warned her that she must always keep this doll with her and never show it to anyone else, not even her father. No one could even know that it existed. If she offered it a small amount to eat and drink in a time of need, it would always come to her aid.

After her mother’s death, Vasilisa’s father wanted to marry again. But the woman he married was cruel, and she and her daughters didn’t like Vasilisa, always burdening her with extra work and chores. But the Motanka doll helped Vasilisa when she needed it. She was kept safe and began to grow ever more

beautiful over the years, which only made the stepmother and her stepsisters hate her even more.

After a time, her father needed to leave on an extended trip. While he was gone, the stepmother sold their house and took up residence at a home near a great birch forest. She burdened Vasilisa with even more work and sent her out into the woods for extra chores and errands, hoping that the evil old witch, Baba Yaga, would find her, kill her, and eat her. Thus, the stepmother and her daughters would finally be rid of Vasilisa while making themselves seem to be innocent. But once again, the doll kept her safe.

The stepmother resolved to find a way to be free of her once and for all, so one night, she crept about the house and extinguished all the candles. "You must go and ask Baba Yaga for more light," the stepmother told Vasilisa. Vasilisa didn't want to go into the woods in the dark, but her doll told her she would be safe. As she walked through the night, a rider in white on a white horse rode past her and then another in red on a red horse, and these two seemed to herald the dawn and the morning sun.

At long last, she came to a strange old house that stood on giant chicken legs and was walled by a fence made of human bones, crowned with human skulls. Sharp teeth locked the main gate. When a rider dressed in black rode by on a black horse and night descended, the eyes of the skulls began to glow. Vasilisa was frightened and wanted to flee, but Baba Yaga returned in that moment, sitting in her flying mortar. "I smell human!" she said. "Who are you?"

Vasilisa told the witch her name and her errand. Baba Yaga replied that Vasilisa could have more light, but first she must stay and work for a bit. "If you do well, I will give you light, but if not, I will cook and eat you!"

Vasilisa agreed, and even though Baba Yaga set for her difficult tasks to complete, Vasilisa's doll was always able to help her complete them, just as it had before. Still, she was forced to serve large amounts of good food to the old witch, who ate generously but gave only bread crusts to Vasilisa. And Baba Yaga grew annoyed that Vasilisa completed all the tasks so well since her true desire was to kill and eat her.

But she allowed Vasilisa to ask her some questions. When she inquired about the riders, Baba Yaga explained that they were the dawn, the sun, and midnight. When Baba Yaga asked how Vasilisa could complete her tasks so well, she replied that she had her mother's blessing. The old witch cringed at the thought of such a kind and holy act.

"I will not have a blessing in my home!" She handed Vasilisa one of the skulls whose eyes glowed, now stuck on the end of a stick. "Here, this is what you came for." She then let Vasilisa leave the strange chicken house and go home.

Vasilisa returned to her house and took the skull lantern inside with the intent of relighting the candles and fires, since nothing now would relight them. But instead of bringing light, the coals in the skull's eyes burned bright and fixated on the stepmother and stepsisters. It began to burn them, and they howled in agony as they were reduced at last to piles of ash.

Vasilisa was unharmed, but she left the house to try her luck elsewhere. She eventually found lodging with an old woman and worked as a clothmaker. The woman was so impressed with her craft that she took the fabric to the tsar, who loved it and wanted to meet the young lady who had made it. So she brought Vasilisa to the palace. The two were smitten with each other at once and resolved to be married.

Soon after, Vasilisa joined the tsar in his palace, and she brought her father and the old woman to live there as well. And she kept the little Motanka doll with her for the rest of her days.

Tatterhood

(Norwegian fairy tale)

Once upon a time, there was a king and queen who loved each other but had no children. So, they decided to adopt a girl whom they loved very much. But one day, the queen saw the child playing with a beggar girl and scolded her. But the beggar girl, who knew the queen had no child of her own, told the queen that her own mother knew a way to change this.

The queen went to the beggar girl's mother and plied her with wine. The mother told her to wash herself with two pails of water at night and then to pour the water under her bed. After this, two flowers would grow, one beautiful and one hideous. The queen was to eat the beautiful one but not the ugly one. The queen did as she asked, and sure enough, the next morning, two flowers grew under her bed, one bright and the other dark. She ate the bright one, and it tasted so sweet that she longed for more, so she ate the foul one even though she'd been told not to.

Nine months later, she gave birth to a daughter, but she was loud and ugly. Even worse, she carried a wooden spoon with her and rode a goat. The beggar girl told the queen that she would have another child who would be beautiful and sweet of temper, and sure enough, she did. And despite their differences, these two sisters were fond of each other as they grew up. The older girl was called Tatterhood because she wore a ragged hood to cover her wild hair.

One Christmas Eve, a great noise sounded outside the queen's chambers. Tatterhood wanted to know what the cause of all the commotion was, and the queen confessed that a group of trolls came to the palace once every seven years and caused strife. Tatterhood resolved to drive them away and told her mother and sister to stay back and keep the door shut. But her younger sister, worried about Tatterhood, opened the door and looked out at the battle. At that moment, a troll tore off her head and replaced it with a calf's head. Tatterhood finally chased the trolls away.

She became determined to restore her sister's head. They set off on a ship and sailed to the island of the trolls. After a pitched battle, Tatterhood was able to capture her sister's head and return it to her. They fled from the island and sailed to another kingdom. There, the king fell in love with the younger sister. But she insisted that she would not marry unless Tatterhood was also taken as a bride. The king's son agreed to marry her, but not without protest.

On the wedding day, the brides-to-be arrived, but Tatterhood remained clothed in her rags and hood while riding her goat. She inquired of the prince why he didn't ask about her goat. When he did, she said that it was actually a magnificent horse, and in that moment, it became one. She then inquired as to why he didn't ask about her wooden spoon, so he did. She answered that it was actually a beautiful fan, which it became in that moment. She asked him again about her tattered hood, and when he responded, it became a gold crown. And finally, she inquired about herself, and when he asked in response, she became a glorious beauty who had been hiding her fair nature for so long. And so, the prince understood who she truly was. He and the king were wed to Tatterhood and her sister, and they all lived happily for the rest of their lives.

The Satin Frock

(Yorkshire folktale)

Once, there was a little girl named Mary. She had a fine satin frock, but her mother gave her a stern warning: If Mary got it dirty, her mother would kill her! It happened one day that Mary was out for a walk when a herd of cows came wandering by. Their hooves kicked up some mud, which splashed on Mary's satin frock. She sat down on a nearby doorstep and started to cry.

The woman who lived in the house heard her and came out to see what troubled her. Mary told her about the dirty frock and what would happen to her if she went home. The woman took pity on her and brought her inside where she washed the frock and dried it. She then sent Mary on her way, telling her to be careful not to get it dirty again.

As Mary walked along a lane on the way home, a horse came trotting by and it splashed her frock with mud again. But now Mary was nowhere near anyone who could help her, and she had no choice except to go home.

When she got there, she confessed to her mother what had happened. She flew into a rage and dragged Mary into the cellar where she cut off her head and hung it up on the wall.

That evening, Mary's father came home and asked where she was. The mother lied and told him that Mary had gone to stay with her grandmother for the night, and this satisfied him.

Later that night, at bedtime, he decided to fetch some sticks from the cellar in order to make a fire.

"No, let me," the mother said.

"No, I will do it," he insisted, and she could not persuade him to let her go down to the cellar instead.

When he arrived there, he saw Mary's head on the wall. After he came back up, he asked about it.

"Oh, it is a sheep's head," Mary's mother lied. "Tomorrow, I will make some broth for our dinner."

And she did just that, serving a broth made from Mary's head.

The father sampled some. "It is a nice broth," he said as he slurped up some in his spoon, "but oddly, it tastes like our Mary."

After he said this, she became very frightened, knowing that she couldn't hide the truth from him any longer. And indeed, when he discovered what she had done to Mary, he dragged her into the cellar and killed her.

My Mother in the Fold

(Icelandic folktale)

Once there was a young woman who lived on a farm. She became pregnant and gave birth to a baby. Now, whether she was married or not no one knows, but she decided that she couldn't and wouldn't keep the child. So, she took it outside far from the farm and laid it out in the freezing cold wilderness so that it would die of exposure. After turning from the child, she put him out of her mind and resumed her life on the farm, attending to her chores and duties.

Sometime later, she was invited to a party where there would be dancing. She would have loved to go, but she didn't have any good clothes to wear, for she was poor. And so, she had no choice but to stay home, where she fell into a bad mood and sulked.

That evening, she went to milk the ewes, something she didn't want to do when she could have been dancing instead. She started to complain out loud about her situation and to lament about not having a fine dress to wear to the party.

Just as she finished her complaint, she heard a ghostly voice wafting through the air, singing a plaintive song:

"My mother, in the fold," the young, innocent voice intoned. "You do not need to be so sad.

For you can wear my old rags, and then you can dance, and dance some more."

A chill went down her back as she recognized the voice. It was that of the infant she had left to die in the wilderness. Numb with fear, she stumbled away, but still the voice carried on. Her murdered child sang out to her, telling her to go and fetch his old rags and to wear them so that everyone could see what she had done.

All of this was too much for the young woman. In her fright and guilt, she fell into a bout of insanity, from which she never recovered.

The Plague Swarm

(Polish folktale)

Once there was a Ruthenian who lost his wife and children to a terrible plague, and to save himself the same fate, he fled from his cottage into the forest and decided to stay there until the sickness had passed from his land. He wandered in the woods and eventually built a small hut and lit a fire. He fell asleep, exhausted from his ordeal.

Sometime after midnight, a loud noise startled him awake. Getting up, he strained to hear more, and soon he made out some kind of song in the distance; it sounded like drums and tambourines accompanying fifes and flutes.

"How can this be?" he wondered. How could people be celebrating when so much death and misery surrounds them? Who could be happy at a time like this?

The sounds grew louder as the merrymakers approached. He hid and tried to spy on them. He saw a multitude of ghosts in a parade, surrounding a large black carriage. They cavorted and played, sang and danced. And on the carriage sat the Plague itself.

And as the procession marched on, it grew in size as everything before it also transformed into ghostly beings that joined the deathly dance. And as they drew near to his little fire, one firebrand still burned. At once, it stood up, and two arms reached out from it, while the fire shaped itself into two eyes. And then, it began to sing as one with the others, a spirit joining the ghostly procession.

The man grew numb with terror. He grabbed his axe and tried to swing it at the nearest specter, but before it struck, the axe flew from his hands and transformed into a woman with long, black hair who also joined in the choir of the damned.

As the swarm advanced ever onward, all life fell before it, such that even trees, foliage, owls, and more transformed into unearthly dancers and musicians, for the plague spared none of them.

He could no longer take in what he saw, and he collapsed, giving in to the lure of death. But then he awoke to the sun shining on his face. All of his meager possessions were ruined, having been taken by the dead, but somehow, he lived! For whatever reason, the swarm had passed him over.

He gave thanks for his life, and leaving that cursed place, he traveled on in search of food and shelter, that he might weather this terrible plague for a while longer.

The Two Corpses

(Russian folktale)

Once there was a soldier who had obtained permission to go on leave from his army duties. He planned to go home and pray to the icons as well as honor his parents. And so, he set off to make the long journey home.

He was still out on the road after sunset, and darkness had descended. It happened that he was passing by a graveyard, of all places, when he heard footsteps behind him as if someone were running toward him.

“Stop!” a rough and evil voice demanded. “You cannot escape!”

He turned to look behind him and saw a hideous corpse lumbering toward him, growling, hissing, and gnashing its boney teeth. Panicking, the soldier dove to one side to avoid its attack and happened to see a small chapel nearby. Without hesitation, he sprung up and dashed for it.

When he got there, he discovered that it was empty, but there was a table in the middle. On that table lay another corpse, surrounded by burning candles. Struck with fear, the young soldier decided to hide in a corner, using the shadows as protection.

Before too long, the first corpse lumbered into the chapel. At that moment, the corpse on the table sat up.

“Why have you come here?” it demanded of the first corpse.

“I have chased a soldier into this place,” the undead creature answered, “and I intend to eat him.”

"No, my brother," the chapel corpse replied. "He has come to my house, so I shall be the one who eats him."

"No!" the first insisted. "I will!"

"No! I will!"

At these words, they began to fight, punching, tearing, growling, and gnashing. Dust flew everywhere, but neither would submit to the other since both wanted to feast on the soldier. They fought for so long that outside, a rooster crowed as dawn came. At that sound, both corpses fell to the stone floor, lifeless once again.

The soldier hurried out of the chapel into the coming morning and gave thanks for being delivered from these two evil creatures, their greedy hunger having saved his life.

The Snow Child

(French/German folktale)

Long ago, there was a merchant who lived with his wife in a simple cottage by the seashore. And while they were comfortable enough, he often had to go away for many months at a time on business. Though they missed each other while he was gone, they had no choice if he was to make a good profit in his work.

So, it struck him as very unusual when he once returned from such a trip to find her at home with an infant in her arms. He had been gone for nearly a year, you see, and he was not happy with this situation.

"Wife, what has happened?" he demanded. "For this child cannot possibly be mine."

"No, dear husband," she answered. "It is not. But do not be angry, for I have never been unfaithful to you, I swear. This boy is a miracle, a Snow Child! This winter past, I was walking home from church when I slipped on the icy road and fell into a snowbank. And somehow, nine months after this accident, I gave birth to this wonder. Is he not splendid?"

The husband had to admit that it was quite a wondrous story, and looking at the baby, he saw that the boy did indeed appear most unusual. He had white hair and white skin like the very snow itself. Satisfied that his wife had not been unfaithful and that they had indeed been visited by a miracle, he agreed to accept the baby as his son.

For some years, the merchant would go out as usual, and he began to think about taking the Snow Child with him on some short trips when he was old enough. One summer's day, he decided to go to a market being held in a nearby village. "I will take the Snow Child with me," he said.

But when he came back that evening, he was alone.

"Where is our son?" the woman asked anxiously.

The merchant lowered his head in shame and sadness. "Something terrible has occurred," he said. "It was hot and we were walking across a meadow in the full sun." He paused for a moment. "And the Snow Child simply melted away. He came into this world in a strange way, and he left it suddenly."

They were very sad but also grateful that they had had the Snow Child in their lives for a little while.

The Griffin's Feather and the Speaking Bone

(Italian folktale)

A king had three sons. But his eyesight was poor from disease, and he brought a physician to examine his eyes. The physician told him that he could cure the malady but that he needed the feather of a griffin to do it. The king summoned his three sons and told them that whoever found the griffin's feather would inherit the kingdom. And so, the sons eagerly set out in search of this rare treasure.

The youngest of the sons encountered an old man who asked him what he was doing. "My papa is ill," the young man said. "He needs a griffin's feather to cure him. He has said that the son that finds it will have his crown."

"Ah," said the old man. "Here, have some corn. You will come to a place where the griffin dwells. Place it in your hat, and the griffin will come to eat it. Then you can pluck out a feather and take it to your father."

The young man took the corn and thanked him, tucking it away until he needed it. He found the griffin, placed the corn in his hat, and sure enough, the beast ate some, and he was able to pluck a feather from it. He placed the feather in his shoe to keep it safe as he went home to the king. But before reaching home, he met up with his brothers, and they asked him if he'd found the feather.

"No," he said, but his brothers knew that he lied. They searched him and finally found the feather in his shoe. They killed him and buried his body, taking the feather to the king and telling him that they had found it. And, true to the physician's word, the feather healed the king's eyes and he could see again.

Sometime later, a shepherd tending his flock saw that his dog was digging into the ground and pulled out a bone. The bone seemed like the right shape for a whistle, so he put it in his mouth to try it. The bone suddenly spoke to him: "Shepherd, keep me in your mouth, hold me tight, and do not let me go! For a griffin's feather, my brothers have been traitors."

Soon after, the shepherd happened to pass by the king's palace, and the whistle again made noises. The king, upon hearing it, asked him what it was. The shepherd let the king try it, and again it spoke: "Father, keep me in your mouth, hold me tight, and do not let me go! For a griffin's feather, my brothers have been traitors."

The king summoned his sons and placed the whistle in the eldest one's mouth. Again, it called out: "Brother, keep me in your mouth, hold me tight, and do not let me go! For a griffin's feather, you two have been traitors."

The king understood what had happened and the brothers confessed. Then he had them put to death for their crime. And thus, sadly, the king had no more heirs.

The Enchanted Pig

(Romanian folktale)

A king went off to war, leaving behind three daughters. He warned them not to go into a specific room, but as soon as he'd gone, they disobeyed him. Inside, they found a book that contained a prophecy. The oldest daughter would marry a prince from the east, while the middle daughter would wed a prince from the west. However, the youngest would marry a pig from the north. Though she was revolted, her sisters assured her that this was not possible.

After the king returned and learned what they had done, he decided to try to make the best of the situation. Sure enough, princes from the east and west did marry the two eldest daughters. And one day, a pig came to court the youngest daughter, but the king refused to admit him. At this, the pig caused the whole city to fill up with more pigs, making a nuisance of themselves. Knowing that this pig was enchanted, the king asked his daughter to go through with the marriage to save the city.

She agreed and married the pig, and upon returning to his home, she found that he transformed into a handsome man each night, which greatly pleased her. She happened once to ask a witch about the man's curse. The witch told her to tie some thread to his foot to free him. She did this one night, only to find that he turned again into a pig. He told her that he was now stuck in this form, and she would not be able to find him again until she wore out three pairs of iron shoes and blunted a steel staff.

She obtained these items and set out to use them up, coming first to the house of the moon. The moon's mother greeted her,

though she didn't know where the young woman's husband was. The mother told her to seek out the sun. She also gave her a chicken and told the princess to keep all of its bones. She departed, having worn out the first pair of iron shoes.

She came to the house of the sun, and the sun's mother greeted her. Her son was bad tempered, she said, and she calmed him down when he returned. The mother didn't know where the young woman's husband was but gave her another chicken with the same instructions to keep the bones. She then sent her away to find the wind. She wore out another pair of the shoes and donned the final pair.

At the wind's house, she met the wind's mother, who told her that her son was in a thick forest. She showed her the way and gave her another chicken, again telling her to save the bones. The young woman walked along the Milky Way and wore out her last pair of shoes.

She found a castle wherein her husband now resided and used the chicken bones to make a ladder to climb. But she discovered that she was one bone short and had to chop off one of her own fingers to complete the ladder. She found her husband and broke the curse. He told her that he was a prince who had killed a dragon. The witch was the dragon's mother and cursed him to be a pig. She'd been deceiving the young woman all along.

He took his revenge on the witch, and then they returned to the young woman's father, the king, in triumph.

The Tale of Scheherazade

(*1001 Nights*)

A great monarch named Shahryār, king of Persia and its surrounding lands, learned that his brother's wife had been unfaithful to him. This disturbed him greatly, but it became even worse when he discovered that his own wife had also been unfaithful. Flying into a rage, he had her beheaded. Now, in his grief, he became convinced that all women were the same and fell into a madness. He decreed that he would marry a virgin each day and have her executed the next morning, and he would continue to do this so that none of them could ever be unfaithful to him again.

His servants carried out this cruel order and brought him a new young woman each evening. She was then beheaded the next day. But at some point, the Vizier could find no more virgins. His daughter Scheherazade volunteered to marry Shahryār, and the Vizier strongly opposed it, knowing her fate, but he reluctantly agreed. For Scheherazade was a clever woman who had a plan of her own.

She had spent much time reading books, chronicles, annals, and legends of her lands and others. She had learned numerous stories, both humble and great. She had learned history and myth as well as poetry, science, mathematics, the arts, and much more. She had become witty, wise, well read, and beguiling.

So, on her wedding night, knowing that the king would kill her the following morning, she asked to say farewell to her sister Dunyazad, and she sat with her telling her a story. Shahryār happened to walk by and hear her tale and became immediately absorbed in it. But Scheherazade stopped before finishing, saying that dawn was coming. He agreed to spare her life for one day so that he could hear the remainder of the tale the following evening.

The next night, she finished the tale for him but began another, also pausing it at dawn and saying she would conclude it the next night. And so, she was able to keep death at bay by telling him new stories each night that she would not conclude until the following day. For the next 1,000 nights, she enthralled him with tales of excitement, magic, and wonder, and each morning, he did not behead her.

After these nights had passed, she told him that she had no more tales. She brought out the children she had borne him and explained that if he were to execute her, they would have no mother and no one else to bring them up. Shahryār was so impressed by all that she had done that he pardoned her and agreed to live happily with her. He gave the Vizier, her father, a beautiful golden robe and ordered that Scheherazade be celebrated throughout the land for thirty days.

And that is how Scheherazade saved herself from the executioner's axe.

The Merchant and the Two Sharpers

(1001 Nights)

A merchant lived in a city called Sendeh. He was quite wealthy and provided good quality merchandise to his customers. He also traveled to other cities to sell his wares, and on one occasion he set out to make such a trip. As he was leaving, two sharpers (that is, swindlers and con men) asked to join him along the way. They pretended to be merchants as well, even though the quality of their goods was not as nice (most of it having been stolen and not well taken care of), but the merchant let them come along.

They traveled for some time on the way to the next city and then stopped to rest for the night. These thieves had already made a plan to kill and rob the merchant. They would take all of his things and slip away. But being dishonest men, they also had each decided to swindle the other, for both wanted to steal all of the goods for himself. But of course, neither knew the ill intent of the other. "If I can cheat my comrade," each thought, "I can have everything and need not share it."

And so, each poisoned the food of the other. The three men sat together eating their meals, and both swindlers ate their poisoned food before either had yet tried to kill the merchant. They sat for a time and talked with the merchant, while the poison in them quietly did its deadly work. They excused themselves from him, going off to plan their next moves, but the poison caught up with them and killed them both.

They were gone for some time and the merchant became curious as to what had happened, so he went in search of them. He found their bodies and realized that they had been con men all along. He reasoned that they'd poisoned each other in their attempts to take his life and steal his goods. But their treachery had instead struck both of them down, just as they deserved.

He gave thanks and then took their goods as well, confident that he could sell some of their wares in the next city since they no longer needed them. Let this be a harsh lesson to all thieves and deceivers!

The Place Where There Were No Graves

(Egyptian folktale)

Once there was a man who had a wife he loved deeply. They were happy for many years, but one day, she died. The man was distraught and didn't know how he could live without her. He began to wonder if there was a place in the world where no one ever died. If so, could he find it?

After he had spent some time grieving, he resolved to set out to discover if such a place existed. He wandered all over the land, searching and hoping that he might yet find a place where death did not hold everything in its cruel grip, a place where people felt no sorrow at the loss of their loved ones. Was there anywhere in this world that had no graves?

One day, he wandered into a land to the south and soon found a town that seemed different. He realized that this town indeed had no graves. Could this be what he was searching for? Was it possible that the sting of death did not touch the world here? He didn't dare to hope.

But he found a local holy man and asked to stay with him. The holy man was very accommodating, telling him not only that could he stay but that he would be able to feast on fine food. That night, they settled down at the table, and the holy man offered him a choice piece of roasted leg.

But the man looked about, wondering why no one else was there to join them in sharing this meal. "Tell me," he said to the holy man, "where is your father?"

The holy man smiled and held up the meat he had just offered. "This is his leg." He pointed to a shelf nearby and said, "The rest of him is up there. Now come and eat with me."

The man learned that in this town, whenever someone fell ill or was wounded, they were killed so that they could be eaten. And that was why there were no graves here.

Terrified, the man ran out the door and kept on running until he returned to his own country. His gruesome discovery led him to accept death and the normal passing of all things.

The Foolish Friend

(The *Panchatantra*, Indian folktale)

Once a great king, while attending to his kingly duties and making various visits, brought along a monkey to keep him company. The king liked the animal very much and always kept him nearby.

The monkey had been spoiled with fine food and was treated very well. Everyone who saw him gave him the same respect that they gave to the king. So much did the king like and respect the monkey that he even allowed him to have a sword, a sign of great trust and friendship.

Near to the palace, the king had seen to it that a beautiful grove was planted, with trees of all kinds. In the springtime, these trees were filled with flowers, which gave off beautiful scents and filled the air with delightful aromas. Countless bees busied themselves with the flowers, flitting to and fro.

One day, the king and his wife went to the grove, and he told his servants to wait at the entrance so that they could be alone. But he did bring his favorite monkey with him.

They strolled about for some time, but the king became weary and wanted to rest. "I would like to sleep for a while in this beautiful place," the king said to the monkey. "Make sure that I am not disturbed."

The monkey agreed, and the king lay down and closed his eyes, soon falling into a deep sleep.

At some point, one of the bees, flying about, alighted on the king's head.

Seeing this, the monkey said, “What? I cannot allow this insect to disturb the king’s sleep, or even worse, to sting him!”

He shooed the bee away, only for it to return. He tried again, but each time he chased it away, it returned to land on the king’s head. The monkey grew angrier, and finally, he drew his sword and struck at the creature. He killed the bee, but his blade also split the king’s head wide open, killing him in one blow.

The queen, who slept next to him, woke up at this, and seeing what the monkey had done, screamed at him. “How could you have done this to the king, who trusted you so much?”

The monkey tried to explain what had happened, but to no avail. Thereafter, he was despised and hated. And so, it is said that it is better to have an enemy who is clever than to have a friend who is foolish.

The Daughter Who Married a Skull

(Nigerian folktale)

A man named Effiong Edem had a beautiful daughter, Afiong. Many men wanted to marry her, but she refused them all. She would marry only the handsomest man in the land, she declared, and he must be young and healthy. The men her father wanted for her were rich, but old and ugly, and so she would not have any of them.

A Skull that dwelled in the land of the spirits heard about Afiong and wanted her for himself. He went about borrowing body parts from several others until he had a complete body, strong and good-looking. He left his own world and came to Afiong's town. He saw her there and became greatly enamored of her.

Now, Afiong heard that a new man had arrived and that he was strong and handsome. She went to see the Skull (not knowing who he was) and fell in love with him all at once. She invited him to her house, and he went there to meet her parents. He asked them if he could marry her, and after some doubts, they agreed. The two married and the Skull stayed at her home for a few days, but then he asked if she would accompany him back to his own country. She agreed, though her parents were not happy about her decision. But her mind was made up, and off they went.

Her father was suspicious and spoke with a holy man who told him that this new husband came from the spirit world, and Afiong would surely die there.

After a long journey, Afiong and the Skull finally entered into his realm. At once, those whom he had borrowed the body parts from came to him and demanded them back. The Skull shed each of his beautiful parts until all that remained was his ugly skull. Afiong was afraid and disgusted and demanded to go home at once, but he would not let her.

They came to the Skull's home, where Afiong met his mother. She was very old and weak, and Afiong tried to help her. And so they became friends. One day, the mother told Afiong that all the inhabitants of this land were cannibals and that, hearing of a new human in their world, they would soon come to the house and kill and eat her. The mother hid Afiong and offered to return her home as long as she agreed to obey her parents in the future.

The Skull's mother asked for the Spider to come and fix Afiong's hair, and then she called up a wind to transport Afiong back to her own land. Afiong's parents were delighted to see her again, having given her up for dead. They celebrated with dancing and a feast, and later the holy man recommended that no one be allowed to marry strangers from faraway lands.

Botan Dōrō, the Peony Lantern

(Japanese folktale)

A long time ago, there lived a widowed samurai named Ogiwara Shinnojō. On the first night of Obon (a commemoration of the dead), he saw a beautiful woman carrying a peony lantern, accompanied by her young servant. At once, Ogiwara was taken with her, and he approached her. When she told him her name was Otsuyu, he asked if she would visit him in his home. She agreed and came to see him. That night, the two made love, and she stayed with him until just before dawn.

Ogiwara was happy when she returned again the following night, with the servant now carrying the same lantern. Otsuyu stayed with him again, and it wasn't long before he fell in love with her. She visited him every night, though she always left just before the light of dawn.

Ogiwara lost interest in others and in anything else, staying home all day and waiting for her to arrive each evening. It was all he cared for; he even neglected himself. And so, this nightly affair continued for almost three weeks. During this time, Ogiwara began to grow weaker with some kind of illness.

Ogiwara's friends grew concerned about him. His next-door neighbor, an old and wise man, happened to hear Ogiwara and Otsuyu laughing together one evening. He decided to investigate, and peering through a small hole in Ogiwara's wall, he saw that the man was in the embrace of a skeleton. Otsuyu had no flesh at all! And when she spoke, a terrible voice sounded instead of that of a gentle young woman.

The old man spoke to Ogiwara the next day and told him what he'd seen. Otsuyu was really a ghost, and Ogiwara needed to go to the nearby temple. He agreed, and once there, he found Otsuyu's grave with an old peony lantern set upon it. The priest warned Ogiwara about her and told him that she was draining him of his life force. He gave Ogiwara a charm to set on his front door, which would keep her away. Ogiwara did as the priest instructed, and true enough, Otsuyu no longer came to his home.

But Ogiwara was unhappy with what he'd done and grew restless. He missed Otsuyu terribly. One night, he got drunk and wandered off to the temple to her grave. His friends eventually found him there in the embrace of Otsuyu's skeleton, dead, but united with her at last.

Hailibu, the Hunter

(Mongolian folktale)

Long ago in Mongolia, there lived a kindly hunter named Hailibu. After each hunt, he would share his takings with his fellow villagers, which made him well liked. Once, while hunting in a forest, he spied a vulture that had a small animal in its grasp. He shot an arrow at the vulture and it let go of its prey, which fell to the ground.

He found the creature, who thanked him. "I am the dragon king's daughter," she said, "and my father will give you a great reward. If you do not want treasure, ask him for the stone that he keeps in his mouth, for whoever puts it in their mouth will understand every animal's language."

"Does such a stone truly exist?" he asked.

"Yes," she replied, "but whatever you might hear from an animal, you must keep to yourself. If you tell anyone else, you will turn to stone."

So, Hailibu went with the young dragon to the seaside. The waters parted and he was able to walk along a path with water pulsing in waves on either side of him. Soon, they came to a magnificent palace, and there he met the dragon king. The king was delighted that Hailibu had saved his daughter and offered him any treasure he might want.

"Might I ask you for the precious stone in your mouth instead?" Hailibu asked.

The king thought for a short time and then opened his mouth and gave the stone to Hailibu. "But remember not to tell anyone

what the animals say to you," the great dragon warned, "or you will turn to stone at once."

Hailibu thanked him and went on his way. Knowing the languages of animals made him a better hunter, and he could provide even more for his village. And so he was content for a number of years.

But one day, he heard some birds talking. "We need to leave now," one said, "for this very night, the mountain nearby will collapse and water will flood the land, bringing death to all."

Hailibu ran home at once and shouted to his village, "We must flee now! We are all in danger!" Unfortunately, the villagers didn't understand why. One old man asked him to explain, since Hailibu had never lied to them. And so Hailibu had to give up his secret. He explained how and why he could understand the language of animals and that the birds had predicted a terrible flood.

But as he spoke, his feet and then his legs began to stiffen and turn to rock. By the time he'd finished, his whole body had become stone, just as the dragon king had warned. His people cried out in shock, but they knew he spoke the truth, and so they hastily packed up what they could, took their animals, and fled. And sure enough, the mountain collapsed and the flood came, wiping out their former home.

Generations later, some spoke of this sad tale and went back in search of Hailibu's stone body, but they have yet to find it.

The Boy Devoured by a Stone

(Tinguian folktale, Philippines)

A little boy named Elonen once sat in the yard outside his house making a bird snare. As if in a challenge, a bird flew by, landed, and called out to him, "Tik-tik-lo-den" ("come and catch me").

Elonen looked up at the bird, smiled, and said, "Have a care bird, for I am making this snare for you!"

Yet the bird ignored this warning and continued to taunt the boy.

Elonen finally finished the snare, and in a flash he threw it at the bird. It caught the little animal and Elonen took it and put it in a jar. Afterward, he went out with other boys to go swimming.

But while he was away, his grandmother, whom he lived with, became hungry. Seeing the bird, she assumed it had been caught for dinner, so she cooked and ate it. When Elonen returned, he discovered that the bird was gone.

"Where has my bird gone?" he asked.

The grandmother admitted that she had taken the bird from the jar and eaten it. When he heard this, Elonen became very sad, so sad in fact that he decided to wander away and never return. He packed up some things and went into the forest. But he could not escape his sadness, no matter how far he walked. At some point, he noticed a large stone jutting out of the ground in a clearing. He resolved that he would end his life there.

“Stone,” he called out, “open up your mouth and eat me.”

The stone obliged and opened its mouth, swallowing Elonen in one gulp.

After some time, his grandmother noticed that he hadn’t returned, and she missed him. She left the house and wandered about, looking everywhere for Elonen but finding no sign of him. She finally ventured into the forest.

Coming to the large stone, she had a sense that the boy was nearby. She tried to open the stone’s mouth, but she could not. She called for horses to be brought to try to pry open the rock by kicking it, but that didn’t work either. She brought out some carabao (water buffalo), but they nearly broke their horns trying to pry the stone open. She had chickens peck at it, which did nothing, and finally convinced thunder to try to rattle open the stone. But nothing worked.

In the end, she had to give up and go home, accepting that Elonen was gone. And all because she had eaten the bird he’d wanted to keep.

The Old Woman Who Was Kind to Insects

(Inuit folktale)

A long time ago, an old woman was left behind in a northern summer campground when her people decided that she was too old to take with them while they searched for new places to hunt. She was so old that she had trouble walking and had only a few teeth left. She couldn't even help with preparing leather for her people to use or to sell to others. So, in an act of cruelty, they abandoned her.

Her own family didn't leave much for her, save for some insects to eat, knowing that she would not survive long on such a meager diet.

But the woman said to them, "I will not eat these poor things just to keep myself alive. While I am old, they are young. Some might be no more than children. I will die before I take their lives just to sustain mine."

Her family didn't care either way, and they left her to her fate. Meanwhile, she freed the insects from the trap that her family had caught them in.

Not long after they were gone, a fox started to hover around her hut. After a day or two, sensing that she was dying, it entered the tent and jumped on her to bite her. The woman now accepted her fate and prepared to be eaten. But the fox did not tear at her flesh to devour her.

Instead, it seemed to be working its teeth on her skin as if trying to remove the upper layers, almost like it was a suit of clothing. And so, the small animal bit and tore, ripped and chewed, removing the woman's skin little by little. But as it worked to pull away bits and pieces, something amazing happened.

The woman was not reduced to bloody meat and bone, but rather she beheld a wondrous sight: underneath her old skin was fresh, new, young skin. As the fox tore away her flesh, a new version of her emerged, and when the animal was done, the old woman now had the body of a beautiful young woman, just as she'd had so many years before. She had been given a new life!

She was astonished, and the insects she'd set free now returned to the hut. They had been so thankful she'd spared their lives that they had asked the fox to help her. He freed her of her old skin so that she might have a new one in its place and be given a second chance at life.

A year later, her family returned, but they found no trace of a body, or even bones, for the old woman was now young again and had left that campground. It was said in later years that she might have gone to live with the insects and married a blow fly who had been kind to her.

The Tímbo Tree

(Guaraní folktale, Paraguay)

Once there was a tribal leader named Saguaa who had a daughter named Tacuaree whom he dearly loved. And while she was devoted to him and their people loved them both, she fell in love with a man from a faraway tribe. She decided that she wanted to go with the man to live with him, and while her father was greatly saddened by this, he agreed to let her leave.

She promised she would contact him when she arrived, but after almost a year had passed, he had not heard from her. He began to grow concerned and feared for her safety, so he set off to the village to find her. But when he arrived, he saw that this village lay in ruins. It had been attacked and its people must have fled. But where?

He resolved to set out looking for her at once. However, no matter how hard he searched, he found no trace of the villagers, and he soon lost any sense of where her trail might have led. He began to feel ill and thought that he could hear her voice somewhere nearby calling to him. He put his ear to the ground, hoping that he might hear the sound of feet walking, anything that might tell him where she and the others had gone. But he heard nothing. Still, he didn't give up, and he kept searching, stopping every now and then to put his ear to the ground again, hoping for some sign, some clue to his daughter's whereabouts. But each time he was met only with silence.

He pressed on, seeking no assistance from anyone and barely minding his own needs. And that would be his undoing. He was destined never to see her again or even know what had happened to her.

Many months later, people from his own tribe found him at last, his dead body lying on the ground. They went to pick it up and take him home, but the body wouldn't move, no matter how hard they tried, so they had no choice but to leave it and bury him there.

Later on, a tree began to grow from his remains, spreading out and reaching high up into the sky. And curiously, when it flowered, its dark fruit looked exactly like human ears. These ears grew on all sides of the tree. It was said that even in death, Saguaa's ears were poised to listen in all directions, forever hoping to catch a sound that might tell him where his beloved daughter had gone. And so that is how the timbo tree came into being, born of a father's love for his daughter and his futile desire to find out what happened to her. He listens for her still.

Boitatá

(South American/Brazilian legend)

Sometime in the past, there was a beautiful forest that hosted all manner of plants and animals. For reasons unknown, a thick and black smoke began to cloud up the sky one day, plunging the forest into darkness. The inhabitants couldn't see the sun during the day or moon and stars at night. Even worse, a heavy rain began to fall and it flooded much of the forest. The animals were forced to take refuge in higher places.

A snake known as the boiguaçu lived in a dark cave and was one of the only animals that stayed behind. He could see well enough in the dark and was able to use that to his advantage. To him, the tastiest part of any living being was its eyes. He

would hunt others and eat their eyeballs, which contained light, making his night vision more and more powerful. His own eyes began to grow ever brighter until they glowed like two small suns.

And his skin began to glow too. It glowed so much that it grew hot and burst into flames. The body of the boiguaçu burned up, but this was not his end. He was reborn as the boitatá. In his new form, he left his cave again to survey the forest. He saw the devastation wrought by fire and flood, and he saw that it had been caused by men who had come to cut down some of the trees and burn the rest.

The boitatá grew so angry that he became like a streak of light, flying over the forest and looking for those who would despoil it. Some of these he set on fire so that they died a horrible death by burning up. With others, he warned that he would do the same if they came back to harm the trees again. Those men, wisely, fled for their lives. They were lucky to escape.

The boitatá and the other animals then set about restoring the forest, which took some time. But eventually, they were able to return it to its former glory, back before the time of smoke, fire, and flood.

And the boitatá remains the guardian of the forest to this day, chasing off or killing anyone who would do it harm. Those that meet this vengeful snake risk being blinded or stricken with madness—that is, if they are not simply burned to death first. If you cross his path, the best way to avoid harm is to stay perfectly still and not even breathe until you can sense that he has gone. But woe to you if your intentions are to harm the forest, for you will certainly meet a terrible end!

La Llorona

(Mexican and Central American ghost story)

There are many versions of the sad and terrifying tale of La Llorona all throughout Central America. This is but one.*

Long ago, a woman named Maria lived in Mexico, and many thought of her as the most beautiful woman in the land. Maria was well aware of this and enjoyed the attention she received as a result. Indeed, almost every day, young men would come to her trying to woo her and even ask for her hand in marriage. But she always turned them down, and they each went home disappointed.

One day, however, she met a man who was different. He came into town, handsome and dashing, and nearly swept her off her feet. She knew at once that he was the man for her, the only one she'd met who could equal her good looks and sophistication. Her other suitors had all paled in comparison.

And so, they were married and soon had two beautiful children. She was happy with him for a short time, but it wasn't long before he began to turn his attention to another woman. And he didn't even bother to do so in secret. This was no affair. Rather, he rode up to Maria one day with this other woman and told his wife that he was leaving her for the newcomer because she was now the most beautiful and elegant in the land. He then rode away, cold and uncaring, with his new love.

Maria went mad with rage and grief. Her heart was broken, and she resolved to do something terrible to take away anything that could remind her of this man. That night, she went to

where her two sons slept and woke them. Taking their hands, she told them to follow her, which they did without hesitation, for why wouldn't they? She led them to a river, telling them that she wanted to bathe them.

But when she guided them into the water, she pushed down on their heads and held them under so that they drowned. Theirs was a terrible and cruel fate, all to rid herself of any recollection of the man she had once loved. Her eyes were full of malice and hate, but after she'd finished the awful deed, she realized how horrific her crime was, and she resolved that she, herself, would share their fate. She plunged into the water and let it fill her lungs, drowning her.

But she found no peace in death, for now her miserable, wailing, vengeful soul haunts the world. She searches at night for other children to replace the ones she lost. And sometimes, she will also murder men in terrible ways as retribution for what happened to her.

*As told by folklorist Camile Acosta

About the Author

Tim Rayborn has a life-long interest in (obsession with, really) the unusual, the strange, the bizarre, and the rather creepy. He has written several books on these topics, including *The Scary Book of Christmas Lore*, *The Scary Book of Valentine's Day Lore*, *The Big Book of Paranormal*, *A History of the End of the World*, and *Beethoven's Skull*, among many others. He's written a huge number of books (over fifty at present!) and magazine articles (more than thirty) on subjects such as music, the arts, general knowledge, fantasy fiction, the whole "weird and unknown" thing, and history of all kinds. He is planning to write more books, whether anyone wants him to or not.

He lived in England for several years and studied at the University of Leeds for his PhD, which means he likes to pretend that he knows what he's talking about. He's also an almost-famous musician who plays many unusual instruments from all over the world that most people have never heard of and usually can't pronounce. He has appeared on more than forty recordings, and his musical wanderings and tours have taken him across the United States, all over Europe, to Canada and Australia, and to such romantic locations as Umbrian medieval towns, Marrakech, Vienna, Renaissance chateaux, medieval churches, and high school gymnasiums.

He currently lives in rainy Washington state with many books, recordings, and instruments.

www.timrayborn.com

About Cider Mill Press Book Publishers

Good ideas ripen with time. From seed to harvest, Cider Mill Press brings fine reading, information, and entertainment together between the covers of its creatively crafted books. Our Cider Mill bears fruit twice a year, publishing a new crop of titles each spring and fall.

CIDER MILL PRESS BOOK PUBLISHERS

"Where Good Books Are Ready for Press"

501 Nelson Place
Nashville, Tennessee 37214

cidermillpress.com